GIRLS
IN SUITS
AT LUNCH

GIRLS IN SUITS AT LUNCH

SCENES FROM REAL LIFE

DEANNE STILLMAN

A DOLPHIN BOOK
Doubleday
NEW YORK
1988

DESIGNED BY PETER R. KRUZAN

Library of Congress-in-Publication Data
Stillman, Deanne.
Girls in suits at lunch: scenes from real life/by Deanne Stillman.
p.   cm.
"A Dolphin book."
I. Title.
PS3569.T482G5   1988   87-27894
813'.54—dc19   CIP
ISBN 0-385-23861-4

To all the guys I've loved before

ACKNOWLEDGMENTS

About three years ago, I was asked by *Gentlemen's Quarterly* magazine to write a conversation in which women discussed men. A one-act play, it was published in *GQ* as *Girls in Suits at Lunch.* I would like to thank Ellen Stern and Art Cooper for giving me that assignment. I would also like to thank my agent, Erica Spellman, who, over lunch one day, heartily agreed that this delightful meal warranted not only eating, but further investigating and publishing as well. Thank you, too, to my editor at Dolphin Books, Paul Bresnick, who is always interested in what the girls two tables over are talking about. In addition, I am very grateful to film director Ruth Charny, a girl in a suit at lunch who managed to sneak away from that event frequently enough to make the short film *Girls in Suits at Lunch* (the first lunch in this book). The film has appeared in the New York Film Festival, Rotterdam Film Festival, and AFI Festival, among others, and often appears on the Arts and Entertainment cable network. Thank you also to Debra Wilkes, who skipped lunch many times in order to type this manuscript. And to my friends and family, who created the world to which over the years I have made many psychic field trips and gone public with my notes, I owe my second greatest debt. The greatest one is to the person who invented *garni*. But lest we forget a man who stands alone in the annals of communication, the Earl of Sandwich—to him, I offer a toast: "You must have been a heck of a guy. Thanks so much for pointing the way toward lunch."

CONTENTS

* Post-AIDS

GIRLS
IN SUITS
AT LUNCH

"Life is funny. Oh dear, oh dear."
—REBECCA COHEN

"Funny ha-ha, or funny peculiar?"
—MANY PEOPLE

"I'll marry the man I love
No other my hand shall claim
For I've given my heart to him, Dad,
And someday I'll bear his name
Remember that gold can't buy
Or conquer a woman's heart
And I'll marry the man I love, Dad,
Tho' from you I part!"*
—MONROE H. ROSENFELD

JANUARY
any year in the 1980s

LUNCH #1

In which Jane and Trish meet to discuss
milestones in their careers, but end up
discussing men.*

Two women in their mid-thirties are having lunch at an
elegant Manhattan tearoom, a shrine to Russian aristoc-
racy popular with the modern workers of the entertainment class who unite here on a daily basis for caviar and
show business theory. The women have known each
other since they were roommates at Barnard, and consider themselves each other's best friend, although like
certain other residents of the late twentieth century,
sometimes they are so busy that they have more contact
with the Eastern European women who muck out American pores for a living than with each other. Both

* Pre-AIDS

women are now "coming into their own," experiencing the kind of success that was always just around the corner. They handle this in the style that is characteristic of their friendship: with a sense of humor that has gotten them through many painful moments.

First, there is Trish Bryant, formerly a dedicated tomboy, now a perfect specimen of physical fitness and traditional prettiness. She has just been made a junior partner in a prestigious law firm. Although perfectly content to listen to Jane talk about her private life, Trish is reluctant to talk about hers. She believes that when women get together for chitchat, they confirm every man's nightmare about what happens when women get together for chitchat, yapping like little dogs with jewelry, squandering the energy of life on notions born of intellectual aphasia: past life therapy, cellulite removal techniques, and male sexual performance. Trish is what was once referred to as a "man's woman," the kind of companion Hemingway would have taken hunting, if only she had a butch haircut. Although she is in her mid-thirties and single, Trish swears that she isn't worried about *that;* she'll get married someday, and if she doesn't, well, she'll survive. After all, some women just weren't meant to live in captivity. Still, she just can't wait to have that next glass of champagne.

She sits across the pink tablecloth and the vase full of fresh peonies from her friend Jane Lazarus. The urbanely attractive Jane is taking Trish out to celebrate her new promotion. In turn, Trish is taking Jane out to celebrate the publication of Jane's second novel, which has appeared to wild critical acclaim. The novel is called *What Gary Did,* and it is a *roman à clef* about Larry, her off-and-on-and-off-again boyfriend of the past six years. To strangers, Jane's calm exterior masks the fact that she is actually an excitable girl. Often excited by her work, which seems to be the only way to make sense out of her complicated life, Jane is just as often excited by her adventures with men, the exciting details of which she divulges whenever she can—sometimes to the world, but always to Trish. Jane, in other words, is what was once referred to as a "woman's woman," the kind of companion Clare Boothe Luce would have validated in *The Women,* if only she were gentile.

Perhaps that's why Jane's passions and accounts thereof secretly excite Trish (yes, our temperaments still reflect religious differences!), but also make her wonder: when Jane swears that she's doing exactly what she always wanted to do, that the only thing getting married means is making out a joint will with a guy who thinks you're lucky to have his last name, even if it's all consonants, does she really mean it? Or is it the mid-thirties' show tune past the official home of the silent majority? As Jane tells it, "The whole world is two glasses of champagne behind." And not likely to catch up, unless Jane slows down—which does not happen at this afternoon's lunch.

TRISH *(raising drink in toast):* Here's to what Gary did. I mean Larry. *(They click glasses in toast.)* Refresh my memory. What did he do, again?

JANE: You'll have to read my book, like everyone else.

5

TRISH: Okay, sorry. Why do you call him Gary? Refresh my memory. I mean, I know that Gary rhymes with Larry.

JANE: I wanted to avoid a lawsuit. Remember?

TRISH: You mean it's okay to say whatever you want as long as you say that Gary did what Larry really did?

JANE: Well, I haven't heard from Larry yet. Maybe he thinks Gary is someone else. Anyway, I thought we weren't going to talk about men today. Remember?

TRISH: You're right. We have to operate on the assumption that there are other things in life. Like—

JANE: Men. *(They laugh and make another toast.)* Speaking of which, I'll be right back. I have to make a call.

TRISH: Couldn't you wait?

JANE: Should I?

TRISH: Even if you should, could you?

JANE: I don't know. Would you?

TRISH *(cxaspcratcd):* Would I what?

JANE: Wait until later to call him.

TRISH: Yes.

(A beat.)

JANE: Okay. It's later. *(She goes to the phone.)*

(The waiter, an attractive, distinctly virile guy who looks too smart for this job, approaches Trish.)

WAITER: Can I get you anything?

TRISH: No, thank you.

WAITER: More water?

TRISH: No . . . thanks.

WAITER: Drink refill?

TRISH: No, I'm fine.

WAITER: Uh . . . Can I ask you a question?

TRISH *(sighing):* Seems to be your M.O.

WAITER: Claus von Bülow—guilty or innocent?

TRISH: What?

WAITER: Personally, I think they should just dust off Old Sparky. How about you?

TRISH: How did you know I was a lawyer? Is this table bugged or something?

WAITER: No. It's something about the way sound travels. I think it's one thousand, one hundred feet per second. Anyway, I overhear a lot of conversations, but I'm always more interested when I hear lawyers.

TRISH: Girl lawyers?

WAITER: Yeah. It helps if they're girls, but I eavesdrop on boy lawyers too.

TRISH: Why? Free legal advice?

WAITER: No, I almost became a lawyer myself and I like to hear what I'd be talking about if I had joined up.

TRISH: Why didn't you?

WAITER: I didn't like the idea of being a hired gun.

TRISH: You seem to have a pretty low opinion of lawyers.

WAITER: Well, it's just my way of saying that I'm different from everybody else in my family.

TRISH: Sometimes I wonder about lawyers myself.

WAITER: Yeah, it's different for women. They haven't had a chance to become famous for going into court and representing white-collar criminals, stranglers, and subway vigilantes.

TRISH: They will.

WAITER: Would you have defended Claus von Bülow if he'd come to you and said— *(responding to a signaling customer)* Excuse me. I'll be right back. *(He leaves. Jane returns.)*

JANE: His line is busy. Anyway, we're here to toast your new job. *(offering toast)* Here's to Hess Barovic Weiss Malign Traduce and Bill. Isn't that the firm that hired you?

TRISH *(with equal sarcasm):* Thanks a lot. I mean, just because we're doing pro bono work for Exxon doesn't mean you have to make remarks like that.

JANE: Sorry. I couldn't resist.

TRISH: It is my job, you know.

JANE: And they did have the good taste to hire you.

(They click glasses in another toast, and order more champagne.)

TRISH: So what did Gary, I mean Larry, do? Come on, Jane, spill the beans.

JANE: Well, he did a lot of things, most of which I found extremely irritating.

TRISH: So why were you with him for five years?

JANE: Six. Because he found my G spot.

TRISH *(incredulous):* There's no such thing!

JANE: Oh yes there is.

TRISH: Where is it?

JANE: Down there somewhere. I can't explain it. Doesn't Robert know what he's doing? Get him to investigate.

TRISH: We're doing just fine, thanks. Anyway, that whole G spot thing worried me. I mean, I don't know if it's such a great idea for women to think that there's another kind of orgasm they're not having.

JANE: Or for men to have to find something new. You know those bras that hook in front? John Kloss for Lily of France?

TRISH: Yeah. I don't like them. They're not very romantic. European women would never wear them.

JANE: Well, I'm American and I'm wearing one right now. Nice uplift, don't you think? *(She cups her breasts to show them off.)*

TRISH *(wearily):* Yes, I think it's generally agreed that your breasts are your best feature.

JANE *(starting to get drunk):* What about my shoulders?

TRISH: Yes, Jane, you have great shoulders.

JANE: Anyway, when I switched from the old kind that hook in the back to the new kind that hook in the front, it took Mike three weeks to figure out how to undo it.

TRISH: Is that why you left him? Refresh my memory.

JANE: No. I left him because I met Pete. Remember?

TRISH: I remember that you never *really* gave me the low-down on Pete. I mean, what *really* happened?

JANE: It took him six months to find my clitoris.

TRISH: I don't believe that.

JANE: Okay, six weeks.

TRISH: Oh, Pete. I remember now.

JANE: I seriously considered publishing a road map. Maybe "two miles north of exit 66" would have been clearer than "higher and to the left." You know—car metaphors.

TRISH: You're a tough nut to crack, Jane. Don't you have anything that anyone can find?

JANE: Personally, I think there should be a new law: two weeks to ring my bell, or the whole thing's off. *(A beat.)*

TRISH and JANE: Three weeks.

(They click their glasses again and take healthy sips of champagne.)

JANE: Hey, that gives me an idea. Instead of prenuptial agreements, you could urge paranoid clients to have sex contracts. The groom relinquishes all claim to his bride's body if cunnilingus is not performed on the wedding night. Is that awful?

TRISH: Yes.

(They have another toast, and order tea sandwiches and another bottle.)

TRISH: So what else did Gary, I mean Larry, do? What else that's not in your book?

JANE: It's all there. If you're too lazy to read it, why don't you listen to the audio version for the blind?

TRISH: Because I know you and I know it's not all there. If you tell me, I'll tell you what Robert and I did last week.

JANE *(wearily):* You fucked in the junior miss dressing room at Saks, and it was the best sex you ever had.

TRISH *(annoyed):* Jane!

JANE: Bonwit's?

TRISH: Look, you haven't heard this story before. All I can say is that it involves electrical equipment, a guy named Julio, and Crazy Eddie's.

JANE *(intrigued):* Okay.

TRISH and JANE: You first.

(They laugh and have another toast, a bit sloppily.)

TRISH: Okay, I'll go. Last Tuesday, when Robert came home from work, he walks in with this long, narrow box wrapped in silver paper with a big red bow inside a Crazy Eddie's bag. I ripped it open and there was this gigantic—

JANE: Uncircumcised black dildo.

TRISH: Well, Robert knows me a little better than that. In fact, he knows me a lot better than that. It was a battery-operated vibrator with three speeds—

JANE: More, more, and more?

TRISH: Jane! I'm telling you a secret! Don't laugh!

JANE: Okay, I'll wipe this smile off my face. *(She mimics wiping a smile off her face.)* So are you and your vibrator registered at Tiffany's now, or what?

TRISH: No—we still haven't resolved our religious differences.

JANE: So where does Julio come in? Don't bother telling me if you mean Julio Iglesias.

TRISH: Well, I have a confession to make.

JANE: Wait! Don't tell me! Julio is "Me and Julio down by the schoolyard"!

TRISH: Jane! I'm trying to tell you something! There is no Julio. I made it up.

JANE: Why?

TRISH: To be provocative.

JANE: Okay. I'm provoked. Tell me the rest of the story.

TRISH: Well, the rest of the story is, I can't tell you the rest of the story.

JANE: Oh, come on. I won't tell anybody.

TRISH: I can't. It's not fair to Robert to go public with our private life. I just can't talk about certain things anymore.

JANE: I guess it's true love between you two.

TRISH *(staring off into space):* Not really. I'm just entering a privacy phase, if that's okay with you.

JANE: Does that mean we won't have anything to talk about at lunch?

TRISH: Why? I can still tell you about my Clint Eastwood fantasies . . . I don't think I'll ever get over his days as Rowdy Yates . . . *(She stares off into space again.)*

JANE: Snap out of it, Trish. Clint's with Sondra Locke-ness now. Anyway, *I* have no immediate plans to stop issuing personal life news flashes. In fact, I may have another one as soon as I make this phone call.

(She gets up and rushes off to make another call. Trish groans. The waiter approaches again.)

WAITER: So, would you have defended Claus von Bülow? The Western Hemisphere is waiting for your answer.

TRISH: No, but I would have had an affair with him.

WAITER: You're kidding.

TRISH: My friend Ruth sat next to him at a dinner party and said he's the most charming man she ever met.

WAITER: Yeah, a real lady-killer.

TRISH: You jealous?

WAITER: No, I'm only jealous of people who seem to have it all figured out.

TRISH: Can I ask you a question?

WAITER: Fire away.

TRISH: Would you have defended Claus von Bülow?

WAITER: Look, our country is based on the principal that a man is guilty until proven he can pay his legal bills or stay off the unemployment lines. *(responding to another customer)* Excuse me just a minute, I'll be right back. *(leaving)* Can you imagine me in court? "Your Honor, can you spare a quarter?"

(Jane returns.)

TRISH: Well?

JANE: Still busy. He's on the phone more than we are.

TRISH: Maybe he's in touch with the female side of his personality.

JANE: Or maybe he's just in touch with females.

TRISH: Don't worry. *"Que sera, sera."* It all works out in the end. There are no accidents.

JANE: You sound like a Celestial Seasonings tea box . . . *(sighing)* I guess that's what happens when you're really in love.

TRISH: I guess so . . . Anyway, it's your turn, Jane. What did Larry, I mean Gary, I mean Larry do? No kidding around this time.

15

JANE: Well, it was more like what he didn't do.

TRISH: What do you mean?

JANE: Well, he didn't like getting head.

TRISH: So that's how you've kept your figure. "The No Blowjobs Diet." Do you think that's Cher's secret?

JANE: Well, it sounds strange, but I really started to miss the feeling of going down on someone. Tom Wolfe once described someone as having "fellatio lips," and ever since then, I've wanted them.

TRISH: Don't ask me. How would I know? I mean, your lips are full, but . . .

JANE: On the other hand, somebody I know has this theory: if God had meant women to give blowjobs, She wouldn't have given them teeth.

TRISH: Jesus, Jane. I think you're, pardon the expression, blowing a good thing. I mean, it sounds like you are completely unable to recognize Mr. Right. Gary, I mean Larry, found your G spot! He laughed at your jokes! He wouldn't come in—or anywhere near—your mouth!

(A beat.)

JANE: I know. I know. "What do women want, anyway?"

TRISH: Another drink, I guess. (pouring each of them a glass of champagne.) So why isn't that in your book? Sounds pretty juicy to me.

16

JANE: Because Gary—I mean Larry—is seductive enough as it is. Why give him free advertising?

(Another beat.)

JANE *(pensively):* I hope we get married soon. I'm tired of introducing people I'm in love with as "my friend." I'm tired of having meals with "friends."

TRISH: Is that a proposal?

JANE: I don't know. I was just thinking. Elaine says married sex is better. Something about not having orgasms in a void.

TRISH: She's probably right . . . On the other hand, what if I actually met Clint Eastwood? Do you think he actually looks as good in person as he did in *High Plains Drifter? Jane drunkenly sings a few bars of the theme from* Rawhide. *They both laugh, but Trish stops laughing first.*

TRISH: Well, at least he's a real man. Unlike Phil "Caller, what's your point?" Donahue.

JANE: What's wrong with Phil Donahue? He's the only liberal on television. Without him, millions of American women would think that Central America is another G spot. You know—

TRISH *(mimicking Jane):* —Down there somewhere.

(They pour more champagne, and order some Earl Grey tea. The tea arrives.)

17

JANE *(taking a sip of tea):* Beverly says we should start exploring the world of younger men, although personally, I find the idea of sleeping with someone who answers to "What's your major?" kind of repellent.

TRISH: Well, she seems contented with Lee.

JANE: That's because he fucks like a bunny and watches MTV all day long, and when he's not watching MTV, he's playing that new laser game called Photon. Not unlike my cousin, who is a senior in high school.

TRISH: Well, I hate to sound like my mother, but "If Bev's happy, I'm happy."

JANE: Well, I guess things could always be worse. Last week I was at this party in Los Angeles and I heard a great, although pathetic, line: Who do you have to fuck in this town to get laid?

(Trish and Jane laugh at this.)

TRISH *(suddenly getting nervous):* Do you think that could ever happen to us?

JANE: Not getting laid? Nah. And if it does, let's make a pact.

TRISH: Okay. We'll never live in Los Angeles.

JANE: No. One of us will get a sex change operation, and then we'll get married. Since you have better eye-hand coordination than I do, and you're already a lawyer, I think it would be much easier for you to learn to live with a penis.

Plus, you'd probably get to appear in court more often. I mean, what do you think the "F" stands for in "F. Lee Bailey"?

TRISH: What about you—every one of your books weighs at least three pounds, and you live like some guy who just got off the boat. I mean, have you ever heard of the vacuum cleaner? You know—that newfangled machine that sucks up dirt? What about that big hunk of metal that heats up and gets wrinkles out of your clothes? I don't think you'd have a big problem with a pair of balls.

JANE: You could be right, Trish. Plus, if the operation were a success, I could become a baseball player and meet Gary Carter—and not just because Gary rhymes with Larry. Then I could find out what male bonding is like . . . Would you get jealous?

TRISH: No, I wouldn't. Quite frankly, Jane, Gary isn't what he used to be. Billy Martin, on the other hand . . .

JANE: Sure, if you could peel him up off the locker-room floor . . . Anyway, I suppose there'd be other problems.

TRISH: You mean like resolving our religious differences?

JANE: No, like wearing teddies. Who would wear the teddy in the family? I don't ever want to give up wearing teddies. Even if I were a man, I would not stop wearing teddies.

(A beat. Trish and Jane realize how silly this sounds and burst into hysterical champagne-induced giggles.)

19

JANE: Look, let's just stay ourselves, okay? I don't want to make out with women—their backs are too small. I like being in bed with men. I like it when they don't shave for a day. I like their smell, except for Old Spice—

TRISH: And Brut—

JANE: And Canoë—

TRISH: And Halston—

JANE: And Paco Rabanne—

TRISH (embarrassed): I slept with a guy who wore Paco Rabanne once . . . Or maybe that was his name.

JANE: Eeyew. How could you?

TRISH: I had a cold. It wasn't so bad.

JANE: You know what smell really turns me on? Paint.

TRISH: You mean you're fucking your super?

JANE: No silly, an artist. He has a lot of cadmium blue on his hands.

TRISH: And he puts them inside you?

JANE: Of course.

TRISH (pretending to be serious): Be careful. Many an artist's main squeeze has been known to end up with a malfunctioning nervous system.

JANE: I'll take my chances.

TRISH: Sounds serious.

JANE: Well, I don't know much about art, but I know what I like.

TRISH: Could this actually be *the* one?

JANE: I don't know. He came over for dinner last night and we had great sex. Do you think I should call him?

TRISH: Well, you've been calling him ever since you got here. I don't see why you're asking me now.

JANE: His line's been busy, so the calls don't count. Do you think I should try again?

TRISH *(signaling for check):* No, don't.

JANE: You're right. I should let him call me. Do you think he'll call?

TRISH: If the sex was as great as you say it was, I'm sure he'll call.

JANE: What if it wasn't so great for him? *(becoming frantic)* Look, Trish, there's plenty of tuna out there, there's a man shortage in this town, or haven't you heard?

TRISH: Jane, take it down a thousand! I'm sure he'll call. But why don't you make a deadline, just to be on the safe side? If he doesn't call by midnight tomorrow—

JANE: Then I can borrow your vibrator? *(more sarcastically)* Great!

TRISH: No, if he doesn't call by midnight tomorrow—

JANE *(seriously): Then* I can call? I don't think I can play hard to get much longer.

TRISH: Listen, Jane, you'll feel better if you don't call. Besides, don't you want to be pursued? You've done everything else!

JANE: But I'm sexually peaking! I've got to call him—

(She runs toward the pay phone. The waiter approaches.)

WAITER: If you'd like to continue this Claus von Bülow discussion, give me a call.

TRISH *(obsessively, like Jane):* What if I call and your line's busy? I'd have to wait and try again. *(embarrassed)* Did I say that?

WAITER: Well, give me your number and I'll call you.

TRISH: I have a boyfriend.

WAITER: Does he like brassieres that hook in the back?

TRISH: I didn't get your name.

WAITER *(leaving to take another order):* Jack.

(Jane returns.)

JANE: No answer. Maybe I should try Gary—I mean Larry.

TRISH: Look, Jane. Maybe this new beau of yours tried phoning you. Ever think of that?

JANE: Good idea. I'll check my machine.

(She rushes off, beeps into her machine, and returns.)

JANE *(continuing excitedly):* He called . . . and says to call back after six!

TRISH: Great! Do you think you can relax now?

JANE *(calmly):* Of course not. *(becoming excited again)* Do you think I should call him back? I mean, maybe I should keep him waiting. You know, play hard to get. Don't you think that's a good idea?

TRISH: I think the best idea is for you to go home, anoint yourself with oils, and prepare for a wonderful evening. He called *you,* remember? Anyway, playing hard to get doesn't work if you're sexually peaking.

JANE: I guess you're right. By the way, Trish, there's one more thing.

TRISH: What is it?

JANE: His name is Larry.

TRISH: Great! Next time I see you and ask "How's Larry?", I won't know who I'm talking about and neither will you.

(The waiter arrives with the check. Jane reaches for it.)

TRISH: Hold on—It's on me. *(She grabs it away.)*

23

JANE *(grabbing it back):* No, but we're here celebrating your new promotion. It's my treat.

TRISH *(grabbing it back):* Wait a minute, you took me out when we celebrated the Pennzoil case.

JANE *(grabbing it back):* And you took me out to lunch when the *Atlantic Monthly* published my article on modern etiquette.

TRISH: No, you took me out when my first objection was sustained.

JANE: And you took me out to celebrate my first book tour. It was your first American Express card.

TRISH: I'd like to consider this the Cliff Notes of your latest work. *(Grabbing check.)*

JANE: Trish!

TRISH: I want to pay. I want to pay. Chalk it up to nostalgia. I remember when you were a starving writer and lived off the free chick-peas at Max's Kansas City.

JANE: And I remember when you were a starving law student and lived off the free wine and cheese balls at freshman mixers.

(She grabs the check and places it face up on the table. Both girls look and do a double take.)

JANE and TRISH: We'll split it.

24

(They empty their purses, looking for their wallets. This takes a solid five minutes. Finally, they pay.)

TRISH: Hey, have a great time tonight—and, not that I need to say it but, let me know what happens. Okay?

(They smile and hug.)

FEBRUARY

SCENE OF THE CRIME

In which Jane and her new beau visit Jane's
hometown.

Jane and Larry are in her new red Chrysler LeBaron
convertible which she bought with the option check for
her novel. They are on their way to Jane's hometown,
Cleveland, Ohio. Although they haven't spent more
than a total of twenty-four hours together, including
about ten in the car, there has been so strong a connec-
tion between them that Jane felt compelled to take Larry
on a tour of her youth. Moreover, as she hadn't been
back in two years, she felt she needed a reality check,
and since she was sexually peaking, she felt that she
might need some sex in the car.

As for Larry—well, he had planned to stay home

this weekend to paint, but this was an excuse not to paint, and also to take a field trip to a city he had been hearing Johnny Carson jokes about for years. Right now, Jane and Larry are heading directly into downtown Cleveland, west to east, eastern bloc to Mayflower descendants, dinner with gravy to dinner with light sauces, on the freeway. On either side of I-90, we see smoke from steel mills, the spires of churches, and billboards that say, "Welcome to the North Coast"; "Cleveland—the best location in the nation"; and "Go, Browns!"

JANE: I always feel like this is the descent into hell.

LARRY: I've heard a lot of Cleveland jokes, but hell?

JANE: No, really. The crosses on those Orthodox churches —look at them! They're not the usual crosses, they're crossed twice.

LARRY: Maybe the Greeks are twice as worried.

JANE: No kidding. Welcome to Cleveland, baby.

LARRY: Well, I've always wondered about this place. I know more comedy writers from Cleveland . . .

JANE *(jealous):* What other comedy writers?

LARRY: Those twins who write for some late-night show, that chick who sells jokes to Rodney Dangerfield, the insulting deejay who just got a book deal—I don't know. Maybe it's something in the water.

JANE: Could be how it starts. Growing up here, you either get into comedy writing or become a sniper. I mean, look at this! The fetid smoke from all these plants! The piles of gravel! A sign that advertises a special on Whitman's Samplers and Tylenol! Who else could have thought of this place but some guy with overgrown fingernails and horns on his head?

LARRY: Jane, are you all right?

JANE: I was okay the minute I left this place.

LARRY: You're sure you're okay?

JANE: Yeah, sorry. I lost it there for a second. I haven't been back in a while. I didn't think I'd get so worked up, but some things never change. *(A beat.)* Anyway, I'm glad you're here.

LARRY: Me too. Even if it does look like hell.

(They start to laugh. The scenery begins to change. They are now on the side of town with trees and no visible sign of heavy industry or religion. This is not Schaefer City; it's where John Cheever would have gotten drunk if he had settled on Lake Erie.)

JANE: Okay, we can roll down the windows now.

(They do. The sun is coming up. It's a beautiful day. Jane turns on the radio and tunes it to WMMS, the station from whence came the assertion that "Cleveland rocks"— which it does. The deejay is spinning Blue Oyster Cult. *Jane*

29

turns it up and accelerates, speeding through this trail of her past.)

LARRY: Hey, this isn't so bad. *(Jane doesn't respond)* Sorry.

JANE: Don't apologize. You're right. It's not so bad. At this very moment, I think I like this place. *(She turns off the freeway, and starts heading for an undisclosed location.)* You see that Big Boy over there?

LARRY: Fried mushrooms and drugs?

JANE: That was the place. It's not so clear which was the better high.

LARRY: Let's stop there and make out.

JANE: Can't. It's all black now.

LARRY: What?

JANE: That's what every white person says about every place they used to hang out at here. "It's all black now."

LARRY: That's wild. I've never heard that.

JANE: That's because you grew up near New York. New York is a melting pot. Cleveland is not. Remember, this is the place where the former mayor turned down an invitation to the White House because it interfered with his wife's bowling night.

LARRY: Hey—watching you behind the wheel is giving me a hard-on. If we can't make out here . . .

(Jane pulls off the road quickly, and the car screeches to a halt on the shoulder of a busy street.)

JANE: How about right here?

(They kiss passionately. Jane starts to unbutton Larry's shirt.)

JANE *(touching Larry's chest):* I could get lost in this tangle of hair forever.

LARRY: I'd like that.

(Jane begins to kiss Larry's belly, unzips his pants, encircling his penis in her mouth until he comes—the moment sweeps through the car like a brush fire. A little while later, they resume the personas known as Jane and Larry.)

JANE: I love to hear your sounds.

LARRY: You make me make sounds I never even knew I had. *(He kisses Jane.)*

LARRY: I owe you one.

JANE: I intend to call it in. That's part of the reason you're here, remember?

(It is now a little while later. Jane and Larry are parked in front of a big Tudor house on a suburban street corner resplendent with magnolias, lilac, and weeping willows.)

JANE: This is it—the house where I spent my formative years.

LARRY: You said it was big, but I didn't realize it was this big.

JANE: It is. Eight bedrooms, twelve bathrooms, I had my own fireplace . . . *(Jane stares at the house for a moment.)*

LARRY: Well, at least you had a little while in a house like this. My parents may still live in the house where I grew up, but there's only one bathroom, and for eighteen years six people used to share it.

JANE: I know there's a toilet joke there, but I don't know what it is because I never make them. Anyway, from what you say, you guys are very close, so it couldn't have been that bad.

LARRY: If it wasn't, why are we all being psychoanalyzed?

JANE: I don't know. Every family has its war wounds. *(A beat.)* Why is it always the suburbs that have weeping willows?

LARRY: Oh-oh. I think I hear a metaphor coming.

JANE: Come on, Larry, don't make fun of me. I'm serious.

LARRY: I know. That's one of the reasons I like you. You're actually a very serious person.

JANE: What are the other reasons?

LARRY: You have bodacious ta-tas. *(He cups one of her breasts.)*

32

JANE *(leaning over to kiss him):* Not now. I'm trying to be serious.

LARRY: I know. *(They kiss passionately.)* Want to call in that IOU now?

JANE: No. I'm trying to extend a metaphor.

LARRY: I think you're succeeding.

JANE: Come on, listen up, here. This is a travelogue of my past, and I want you to pay attention.

LARRY *(snapping to attention):* Okay, Sergeant Jane. I'm all ears, sir—er, ma'am. *(He salutes.)*

JANE: Anyway, as I was saying, I have this theory that weeping willows are indigenous to the suburbs because there's so much sadness in the houses.

LARRY: What about all of those happy barbecues? Just kidding.

JANE: Well, I suppose you're right in one way. Every time I visit Cleveland, I sit in front of this house and stare at it for a few minutes. There must have been something I liked.

LARRY: Besides having your own fireplace, what was it?

JANE: I guess it was the birthday parties. I've always loved my birthday, which, by the way, is next week—

LARRY: So you've announced.

JANE: And I guess maybe it's because my parents always made it seem like a national holiday, and it all used to happen in this house.

LARRY: Looks like a great house for a party.

JANE: It was. When you come in the front door, there's this long marble hallway, and then there's this big round room with mirrors on the walls, and of course, the floor's still marble here—perfect for receiving guests!

LARRY: I'll drink to that—let's go have one.

JANE: But it's not even cocktail hour.

LARRY: I know, but hometowns always make me want to have a drink. Even if they're someone else's.

(It is now twilight. Jane and Larry are in a cemetery, standing before a simple, granite marker. This particular cemetery is in the heart of Little Italy, and so the souls of the dead will forever rest in peace, knowing that the only disruption in the neighborhood is annual and brief—the Calzone Cook-Off in honor of San Gennaro at the end of the summer.)

JANE *(to grave):* Grandma, this is Larry. *(in high-pitched voice of old woman)* Hi, Larry.

LARRY: Oh, hello, Mrs. Lazarus. *(to himself)* Am I really doing this?

34

JANE: Grandma, I know this is unusual, but for some strange reason I just wanted you to meet my friend here.

(Grandma speaks in a voice-over that only Jane can hear.)

GRANDMA: Can you get him to stand a little closer? I can't see.
(Jane motions for Larry to move closer to her.)

JANE: Don't you think Larry is handsome?

GRANDMA *(loudly)*: Didn't I meet someone named Larry a couple of years ago? Same height, a Yankee fan . . .

JANE: Grandma, keep it down.

(Larry looks at her strangely.)

JANE *(shrugging impishly)*: Sorry. Sometimes Grandma gets a little excited. As a Jewish princess from Vienna, she wasn't really prepared to be buried quite so near stores that sell plastic figurines of sobbing saints.

GRANDMA: I wasn't.

LARRY: Look, uh, maybe I better just wait in the car for you. I'll take a walk.

JANE: No, it's okay, really.

LARRY: You two ladies need some time to yourselves, I can tell. Excuse me, Mrs. Lazarus. Nice to meet you.

JANE *(in voice of Grandma)*: Nice to meet you too, Larry. Maybe next time you can stay and have some kugel.

35

(Larry walks off quickly.)

GRANDMA: So, what's with Larry number 2?

JANE: Can't you wait until he's out of earshot?

GRANDMA: He can't hear me. Only you can. Remember?

JANE: You don't realize how penetrating your voice is. Even from the beyond.

GRANDMA: Well, if you would come and visit a little more often, I would probably speak in a more normal voice. I'm excited. I yelled. So sue me.

(A beat.)

JANE: What kind of a vibe did you get from Larry?

GRANDMA: He loves you. True, he's one of those modern fellows who has trouble making a commitment. Too many options in the eighties. Too much tuna. Am I right?

JANE: I don't know.

GRANDMA: What do you mean, you don't know? A girl gets a feeling in her kishkes, you know what I'm talking about. I mean, is this mensch material, or what?

JANE: I think so, but I think he's afraid to think so.

GRANDMA: What kind of a mensch is that?

JANE: A mensch with too many options.

GRANDMA: What's with you and your crowd anyway? Can't any of you get these guys to settle down?

JANE: Grandma, you're missing the point. So far, it's been my choice not to get married. It was never a goal of mine to be called "Mrs." On the other hand, do you think it's strange that I sound like a parent when I talk to my cats? I mean, the other day, when they were fighting in my bedroom, I told them to "pipe down in there."

GRANDMA: Well, I never got it—this career-woman gang of yours. What kind of a legacy is paying off a condo?

JANE: What kind of a question is that?

GRANDMA: How's your friend Trish? Is she married yet?

JANE: She's fine.

GRANDMA: Which means she's not married.

JANE: That doesn't mean she has cooties.

GRANDMA: In my book, she has cooties. Do you two girls plan to spend your lives in suits having lunch?

JANE: Lunch is better than it used to be, Grandma. There are more forms of lettuce.

GRANDMA: Yeah, yeah, I know. Radicchio. Sometimes it's grilled. So, since when is eating warm salad with girlfriends more important than having a man?

JANE: Grandma, that's not exactly what it all comes down to.

GRANDMA: Everything comes down to that, Jane. Now let's get back to this fellow Larry. Easy name to remember. Have you met his people?

JANE: No. I'm going to next week. They're in Syracuse.

GRANDMA: Syracuse? Ask them if they know the Rokeaches. Good family. If they do, my advice to you is to string Larry along until he produces the ice.

JANE: Ice? Isn't that awful?

GRANDMA: Awful? I'll tell you what's awful. Choking to death because you can't perform the Heimlich maneuver on yourself. That's what happened to me. You know—

JANE: Grandma, the Heimlich maneuver wasn't around when you died.

GRANDMA: Well, you know what I mean. I should have married Sol Levin after your grandfather died, but I was too proud and I thought that I would be able to face life alone.

JANE: You did.

GRANDMA: That I did. But death was the hard part. Don't die alone, Jane.

JANE: But what if my husband is out having his pacemaker rotated, and I die then? You never know.

38

GRANDMA: Jane, you've got to give it your best shot. Trust me on this. If there's anything I've learned, it's that dying alone is about as much fun as a screen door in a submarine.

JANE: How do you know that expression?

GRANDMA: I'm dead. I know everything.

JANE: Then tell me what it's like on the other side.

GRANDMA: It's not so bad. I'm finally dating Sol Levin. He says I look just like I did twenty years ago—which is the last time I saw him.

JANE: Well, thanks for the advice, Grandma. See you soon.

GRANDMA: Good luck with anybody named Larry, especially this one. You got gold there, I can tell. And speaking of jewelry, any trick you can think of to get that diamond out of Larry, use it. Just remember one thing! It comes with a curse.

JANE: What curse?

GRANDMA: Larry.

JANE: I love you, Grandma.

GRANDMA: Kowabunga, Jane.

JANE: Kowabunga?

GRANDMA: You know, hang loose. I told you, I know everything.

(It starts to rain and Jane races back to her car, and Larry.)

MARCH

WHO'S THE MOM AROUND HERE?

In which Trish gives her single mom dating advice.

We are inside the traditionally furnished suburban living room of Trish's mother's house, which is in Chappaqua, New York. This is the house in which Trish grew up and nothing here has changed, even the location of the wastebaskets which over the years Mrs. Bryant meticulously decoupaged. Even the family dog, Jude (as in "Hey, Jude"), which Trish named for the Beatles song when she got it, in human years now obviously quite old for a dog, sleeps in front of the beanbag chair. In fact, of course, there is something "wrong" with this picture— Mr. Bryant doesn't live here anymore. He and Trish's mother divorced somewhat amicably several years ago, a swinging couple whose point of rendezvous evaporated when Mrs. Bryant renounced gin and tonics and went on a diet.

Instead of quietly playing light classical music, the record player is playing Van Halen. Trish's mother stands in front of the speakers, a severe expression on her face. Trish walks in through the front door.

As many grown-ups do when they return home, Trish immediately becomes a child, exploring the refrigerator for leftovers (and always finding a meat loaf in one stage or another of consumption); asking for permission to stay out late; and wondering whether or not she's going to be cited for good or bad posture. However, now that her mother is dating and thus in need of a parental unit herself, Trish is confronted with a situation in which Mrs. Bryant is so preoccupied with her own sex life that home may no longer be the repository of tuna salad sandwiches without the crusts that it once was. Not that Trish really wanted a tuna salad sandwich without the crusts, but just in case . . .

TRISH: Mom, what's going on in here? I could hear that music when I pulled into the driveway!

MOM: Sshhh! I'm trying to listen!

TRISH: Listen to what?

MOM: Listen to the lyrics. Listen to "Why Can't This Be Love?" I've listened twelve times, and I don't think he ever really says why.

TRISH: Mom, are you in love?

MOM: Be quiet. I think this is the part where he might explain it.

(Trish stops talking, and Mom listens intently.)

MOM: Maybe there's something I'm just not getting.

(Trish turns down the record player and sits down.)

TRISH: What is going on with you?

MOM: Did you bring the leather jacket?

TRISH: Yeah, I brought it.

MOM: Oh, goody!

TRISH: Van Halen, my leather jacket, "Oh, goody!"—Mom, has your body been possessed by a disc jockey from outer space?

MOM: I'm just having a little fun, dear.

TRISH: You never thought heavy metal music was fun.

MOM: It's not heavy metal. It's thrash music.

TRISH: Thrash music?

MOM: It's louder and faster and more intricate than heavy metal. You may think that heavy metal peaked with "Stairway to Heaven," but I guarantee you, the best is yet to come.

TRISH: Mom, I think we better talk.

MOM: I'm supposed to say that.

TRISH: You haven't said that in years.

MOM: Well, I used to say it.

TRISH: I guess you never listened to what you told me during those talks.

MOM: What do you mean?

TRISH: What I mean is . . . I can tell by the look on your face that you're involved with somebody, and I want to know who it is!

MOM: You sound like a parole officer! I'm not some kind of ex-con who has to check in every week!

TRISH: Then why do you want my leather jacket?

MOM: I've borrowed your clothes before.

TRISH: The only thing you've ever borrowed is my Perry Ellis coat.

MOM: That's not true. I borrowed your Spitalnick camisole. Remember?

TRISH: Oh, yeah. That's true. And you borrowed my pink rayon harem pants.

MOM: What pink rayon harem pants?

TRISH: The Anne Pinkerton pink rayon harem pants.

44

MOM: They weren't pink. They were rose.

TRISH: Come to think of it, where are they?

MOM: They're at the dry cleaners.

TRISH: Why? You can hand-wash rayon. It's cheaper.

MOM: They weren't rayon. They were silk.

TRISH: Mom! Don't you think I'd know if I had silk harem pants?

MOM: Well, dear, there are so many things one must know in order to function in the modern world, it wouldn't surprise me if it just slipped your mind, like forgetting to phone Aunt Helen the other day.

TRISH: I did too phone Aunt Helen the other day. The line was busy.

MOM: Why didn't you call back?

TRISH: I, uh, forgot.

MOM: She's never forgotten you when you were in pain. Every scraped knee, every time you had a cold—

TRISH: Mom, all she did was break a knuckle!

MOM: Two knuckles.

TRISH: All right. I'll call. In the meantime, do you think you could refrain from acting like a parental unit for just a second, and tell me exactly why you want to borrow my black leather jacket?

MOM: Now who's acting like a parental unit?

TRISH: It's just girl talk, Mom. Now give me the lowdown. Got a hot date?

MOM: Well, as a matter of fact, I do.

TRISH: What's his name?

MOM: Allen.

TRISH: Allen what?

MOM: Allen McDermott.

TRISH: And how old is this Allen McDermott?

MOM: Do I ask you how old your beaux are?

TRISH: Mom, how old is he?

MOM: Well, he's a grown man, dear.

TRISH. Did you say grown or growing?

MOM: He's your age, dear.

TRISH: Where do you meet men my age? A lot of women my age have trouble meeting men my age.

MOM: I met him on jury duty.

TRISH: So that's why you were excited about being sequestered.

MOM: No, that's not why. I was excited about being sequestered because I was grateful for the opportunity to finally see how the American jury system works. I am happy to report that it works just fine, and we are very lucky to live in a country where everyone bends over backward to listen to the defendant's story.

TRISH: Does that mean you got laid?

MOM: Trish!

TRISH: Well, does it?

MOM: Not that it's any of your business, but I would never go all the way on a first date.

TRISH: Me neither.

MOM: You used to.

TRISH: How do you know?

MOM *(singsong):* Remember Captain Penny? Your favorite TV show?

TRISH AND MOM: "You can fool all of the people some of the time, and some of the people all of the time, but you can't fool Mom."

(They laugh.)

TRISH: So was jury duty the first date?

MOM: Sort of. Allen and I were attracted to each other as soon as we made eye contact in the jury pool. After I had read the newspaper for the tenth time that morning—incidentally, my horoscope predicted this whole thing—I got up, walked past Allen to the drinking fountain, and accidentally on purpose dropped my clutch bag in front of him.

TRISH: Mom, that's so manipulative!

MOM *(proudly):* I know. You modern gals should try it sometime.

TRISH: Then what happened?

MOM: Then we started talking, got picked for the same jury, and we spent the next week together at the Criminal Court building.

TRISH: You mean jurors shack up while they're deliberating the fate of others?

MOM: Not exactly. The night that we were sequestered, they put us up at the Skyline Motel. Boys stayed with boys and girls stayed with girls. It was just like camp, except instead of campers, the place was swarming with hung juries.

TRISH: Speaking of hung—

MOM: All right, young lady, that's enough. You always did have a smart mouth.

TRISH: Come on, Mom. You're not getting out of this.

MOM *(blushing):* Well, I honestly don't know, dear. To-night's just our second date.

TRISH: Well, don't rush into anything.

MOM: Do I look like I've rushed into something?

TRISH: No. Not at all. Just because you've suddenly become the world's foremost expert on heavy metal—

MOM: Thrash music.

TRISH: —on heavy metal music, when for the past fifty-seven years, your idea of a wild evening was Ella Fitzgerald, well, that doesn't make me think you're rushing into anything at all.

MOM: Good. *(changing subject)* How's Robert these days?

TRISH: Mom, don't change the subject.

MOM: The subject is men, and your mother asked you about the man in your life, and when she asks you a question, she expects an answer.

TRISH: All right. Robert is, uh, Robert is, uh, Robert is moving . . . to another city.

MOM: Is that bad?

TRISH: I don't want to discuss it.

MOM: Why not?

TRISH: I'll sound like a magazine article about the plight of single women in their thirties in the eighties. I don't want to be part of a sociological trend. It's too boring.

MOM: Isn't there safety in numbers?

TRISH: No, just claustrophobia, anonymity, and loneliness. Any other comforting homilies?

MOM: You baby boomers are a confused bunch of children, I must say.

TRISH: Well, get used to it. You're dating one of them.

MOM: I guess you're right. But Allen seems so mature for his age. He's had the same job for ten years—

TRISH: Which is what?

MOM: He's a sound engineer at Spin Studios. He just laid down the tracks for Ashford and Simpson's new album.

TRISH: "Laid down the tracks?"

MOM: Don't you know what that means?

TRISH (exasperated): Yes, I know what that means!

MOM: And he served in the army during Vietnam—

TRISH: You're going out with a Vietnam vet? Okay, never mind the fact that he either wasn't smart enough to beat the draft or felt that we should nuke the gooks, what if he's some kind of walking time bomb, or maybe he's got Agent Orange disease, which is degenerative, in which case you're falling in love with a rutabaga. Mom, what's with you?

MOM: Trish, settle down! First of all, Allen was a radio operator for a team of medics during Vietnam, not some trigger-happy soldier who wanted to nuke the gooks. Second of all, the mind cannot always tell the heart where to lead it. And third of all, if Allen is a rutabaga then Robert is, well, Robert is Mr. Potato Head. So there.

TRISH: Are you in love?

MOM: I don't know. Yesterday I started daydreaming about Allen, and instead of cleaning with Mop & Glo, I washed the floor with Shake 'n Bake.

TRISH: I felt like that when I first started dating Robert. I was supposed to meet him at the Rib and Reef, but ended up at the Ship and Shore.

MOM: When Allen and I played footsie under the table in the jury deliberation room, I thought I would fettuccine Alfredo in my pants.

TRISH: Mom!

MOM: Well, I'm still ripe on the vine! I have a right to my own sex drive.

TRISH: I guess it's hard to stop thinking of you as the person who keeps telling me to join the Clean Plate Club, even though you're going out with a Vietnam vet heavy metal freak—

MOM: It's thrash music.

TRISH: Sorry. Thrash music. Where are you going, anyway?

MOM: Out to hear some thrash music.

TRISH: Out where—somebody's paneled basement?

MOM: No, the Arena. Ozzy Osbourne is in town. We're the third stop on his world tour.

TRISH: I heard that's been sold out for months. How did Allen get tickets?

MOM: He's on the guest list. We're going backstage!

(Trish produces the leather jacket. Her mother quickly grabs it and puts it on.)

TRISH: That looks hot, Mom.

MOM: Really?

TRISH: Really. But I'm not so sure if it goes with the rest of your outfit.

MOM: This linen ensemble from Peck & Peck? I thought the contrast was cute.

TRISH *(taking in the look):* On second thought, you're right. It's completely you. Move over, Valerie Bertinelli.

MOM: Who?

TRISH: She's married to—never mind.

(The doorbell rings. Excitedly, Mom opens it. There stands Allen McDermott in full heavy metal dress. He makes the two-pronged devil sign with his hand. Mom motions him in.)

MOM *(good-naturedly):* Don't rush me, sweetie.

(Trish reacts to Mom's use of the word "sweetie.")

MOM: Ozzy Osbourne is one thing, but I don't know if I'm ready to worship at the altar of Mötley Crüe.

TRISH and ALLEN: Judas Priest.

(Trish and Allen start laughing.)

MOM: What's so funny?

ALLEN: You must be Trish.

TRISH: Hi, nice to meet you, Allen. I feel like I should ask you if you have car insurance.

ALLEN: I don't. I ride a motorcycle. *(off Trish's look)* Don't worry. It's insured.

TRISH: I hope you have a helmet for Mom.

(Allen produces one.)

MOM: Wow! We're really going in style.

TRISH: Well, you kids try to get home at a reasonable hour, okay? *(Mom gives her a dirty look.)* Just kidding. Have a great time, really.

(Allen and Mom start to leave. Allen is out the door first. Just before Mom vanishes for the evening, Trish takes her aside.)

TRISH *(offering cash):* Mad money.

MOM *(refusing it):* Trish!

TRISH: Just in case. You never know.

MOM *(accepting the money and putting it in one of the pockets of the leather jacket):* Thanks. But don't worry. I'm not planning on getting mad.

TRISH: Well, all right. He seems like a nice fellow. But if he tries to pull any fast ones, you just tell him where to get off . . .

(Trish gives her mother the two-pronged devil sign).

MOM: . . . "Young lady."

(They giggle and then kiss good-bye. Trish turns off the Van Halen record and we hear a motorcycle roar away. Trish picks up the phone and dials.)

TRISH: Hello, Jane, I think my privacy phase just wore off. Right now, my mother is sitting on top of a motorcycle wearing a leather jacket on her way to the Ozzy Osbourne concert . . .

APRIL

QUEST FOR ECSTASY

In which Jane and her steady boyfriend
ponder the flight path of passion.

It is now several months since Jane and Larry have been
dating. They have been seemingly happy for the most
part, until Larry received a letter from an old girlfriend
and started telling Jane to stop dressing like a teenager.
He also started telling her to lose five pounds and stop
laughing at her own remarks. In response, Jane, whom
Larry fell in love with in the first place because she
dressed like a teenager, had a very grabbable extra five
pounds, and appreciated her own remarks so much that
she often giggled out loud upon making them, tele-
phoned an old flame with a ranch in Wyoming, and
started to wish that Larry did something else besides

make art, despite the fact that much of his art work reflected the passion in their relationship. Jane and Larry have just seen *9½ Weeks* at a Kim Basinger festival (her comment: "What's that—something that lasts for nine and a half minutes?"), an activity that brings up the problems in their relationship. They are having dinner at a place where the cost of none of the entrees is less than their respective ages.

LARRY: Can you believe how beautiful Kim Basinger is?

(A waiter arrives to take their order, overhearing Larry's remark.)

WAITER: She's no Jean Harlow. What would you like to start with?

JANE: I guess I'll have the salmon mousse.

LARRY: I'll have the puff pastry with morels in vermouth sauce.

JANE: Larry, you hate vermouth.

LARRY: Vermouth is great with morels.

JANE: Is that what they taught you in Syracuse?

LARRY: It was more than you learned in Cleveland.

WAITER: Whew! Dial nine-one-one! Entrees?

JANE: How tiny is the tiny game bird?

WAITER: Don't share it.

LARRY: I'll have the steak frites, medium rare, lots of frites. And could we have a bottle of the house wine, the red?

(The waiter writes down their orders and then moves off.)

JANE: So what's so unbelievable about how beautiful Kim Basinger is? Lots of women are beautiful. We even know some of them.

LARRY: She moves like an animal.

JANE: But those aren't her own moves. A director is telling her to do that.

LARRY: No. You can't tell anyone to move like that. It's completely natural.

JANE: You never tell me that I move like an animal.

LARRY: Yes, I do.

JANE: No, you don't. Why don't you ever tell me that I move like an animal? Don't you think that I move like an animal?

(The waiter arrives to pour the wine, and overhears this remark.)

WAITER: Everybody does—under the proper conditions. *(He pours the wine.)* Here's to the proper conditions.

JANE: You can tell me the truth. I'm a grown-up. I'm not going to drop dead if you tell me that you don't think I move like an animal.

LARRY: Well, sometimes you move like an animal.

JANE: When? *(A beat.)* Look, Larry, just tell me the truth. Do I or don't I move like an animal?

LARRY: What do you want to move like an animal for?

JANE: Do you know that Kim Basinger had her lips done?

LARRY: What's that got to do with it?

JANE: I heard that she had them made more pouty in order to get that part in *9 1/2 Weeks.*

LARRY: God, she was hot! Remember the scene where she's sitting naked at the dining-room table?

JANE: It was the kitchen table.

LARRY: And Mickey Rourke caressed her with a red pepper?

JANE *(turning the tables):* Yeah, vegetable sex. *(A beat.)* I kind of liked that too. I'd let him caress me with anything, any time, any place, anywhere, with anything.

LARRY: What?

JANE: If there's one person I'd let fondle me with roughage, it would be Mickey Rourke.

LARRY: What's so great about Mickey Rourke?

JANE: I don't know. I think it's because he talks like this *(imitating him)* all the time.

LARRY: But you can't understand anything he says.

58

JANE: So? Kim Basinger isn't exactly a communications major. On second thought, I bet that *was* her major, at junior college.

LARRY: If you want to discuss great minds of the twentieth century, let's move on to your one-and-only—Nick Nolte. What happened to him—too fat?

JANE: I heard he was totally wrapped up with Jackie Bisset.

LARRY: I heard he had gravel implants put in his larynx so he could get the part in *48 Hours.*

JANE: Touché.

(A beat.)

JANE: Larry, have you ever wanted to slather me with honey, throw me across the pantry, fuck my brains out and then kill my husband?

LARRY: What movie is that?

JANE: What difference does it make? Have you ever wanted to do any of that?

LARRY: Okay, I'll just jump right in here. First of all, you don't even have a husband.

JANE: But if I did, would you want to kill him?

LARRY: What kind of question is that?

JANE: I mean, do you want me, no matter what?

59

LARRY: What?

JANE: I mean, what if I were being held hostage by some terrorists with towels on their heads? Would you do anything to get me out, or what?

LARRY: You know that I believe terrorists should be taught a lesson, no matter what they are or are not wearing on their heads.

JANE: What if I were pregnant?

LARRY *(scared):* Are you?

JANE: Maybe.

LARRY: Look, Jane, I've told you. I don't see any point in reproducing. I thought there was some hope for a while but then the summit talks in Reykjavik fell apart, and well, I just don't see the point. So if you're pregnant—

JANE: It's always something with you. Last time we talked about this, you said you were waiting until they gave you an unlimited line of credit at Master Charge.

LARRY: Well, babies are expensive.

JANE: Look, Larry, I'm not pregnant. But I'm starting to feel like Captain Hook with this clock ticking away. Tick-tock, tick-tock—

LARRY: Don't overdramatize. Britt Ekland just had a baby.

JANE: And she's pushing fifty. Imagine that!

LARRY: Well, she looks pretty good to me. I mean, not as good as Kim Basinger, but—

JANE: What are you saying, Larry? That I should wait until I'm fifty before having a baby?

LARRY *(apologetic):* No, not really. What I'm really trying to say, I guess, is that, uh, we should start seeing other people.

JANE *(trying to take it "like a man"):* Do you have a date with Kim Basinger?

LARRY *(bad joke):* I tried, but I guess her service never gave her the message.

JANE: You never did know how to use sarcasm properly. There's a time and place, you know.

LARRY: I thought that was pretty funny myself.

JANE: Look, I'm the funny one around here. "When in trouble, use your sense of humor. That's your best quality." You told me that once, remember?

LARRY: Yeah, well maybe I was just trying to be funny. *(A beat.)* Maybe if you'd use a little less sarcasm some of the time, and stop acting like nothing bothers you, we'd have a better relationship.

JANE: You mean we should be more like Rachel Ward and Burt Reynolds in that movie where he rescues her from a life of prostitution and less like Tracy and Hepburn in all of those movies where they fondle each other with their clever rep-artee?

LARRY: Something like that. Look, all I'm saying is maybe we need a break. Let's call it something less final—a leave of absence.

JANE: I can't believe this. The first week I met you, you insisted that I meet your entire family, which happens to be half of Syracuse.

(The waiter arrives with the appetizers.)

WAITER: Life *is* Syracuse, honey. Better get used to it.

(He puts them down and leaves.)

LARRY: And you transported me across interstate lines to meet your family. I'm sure that was a violation of some statute.

JANE: You didn't actually meet members of my family. You visited various shrines of my past. I felt it was too early in the relationship for you to have to deal with actual relatives.

LARRY: I'm just not as secretive as you are. Everyone knows everything I'm doing, relatives included.

JANE: Why not? You don't do anything serious. You don't need to have secrets. It's always "Welcome aboard" time with you, which is your way of avoiding me.

LARRY: What?

JANE: Sometimes when I ask you if we can go to the movies alone, you act like I'm asking you to help me pick out a dishware pattern at Tiffany's.

LARRY: Oh, come off it.

JANE: Then sometimes you're just the opposite. I feel like while we were in Syracuse, you and your family of energy vampires were all over me, like I was a vestal virgin. I've needed a blood transfusion ever since. Then, on the train back from your brother-in-law's, you were in seventh heaven when we could pretend we were married in order to get that Amtrak couple's discount. I haven't seen you that excited since you showed me your old paper route. What's with you?

LARRY: I don't know. I wanted it to work. But it's not.

(A beat.)

JANE *(mulling it over, then switching gears):* I know. You're right. We do need a break. Not a leave of absence.

LARRY *(surprised):* We do?

JANE: Well, I have a confession to make.

LARRY: You've been seeing someone else.

JANE: I've been seeing someone else.

LARRY: Who—your editor? You're always talking about him.

JANE: That figures. Men always think the person to worry about is the one the girl's always talking about. Anyway, yeah, he's cute, like my editor, but I'm way past the mentor stage as far as romance goes.

LARRY: What's with this "men always do this and that" business? I thought we agreed never to talk about each other like typical members of the opposite sex.

JANE: Well, you're acting like a typical member of the opposite sex. To reiterate, whenever I ask you about dinner tomorrow night, you start acting like I've just asked you to make out a joint will.

LARRY: I've never acted like a typical man with you, whatever that is.

JANE: Well what about dinner tomorrow night? Gordon and Susan want us to come over, and you've been avoiding the subject for a week.

LARRY: I don't know. Tom's coming in from Syracuse. I haven't seen him in three weeks. I'm just telling you the truth.

JANE: I know you're not lying. But how come whenever you're at my house, you feel free to pick up my phone and answer it, and when I'm at yours, you act like the phone is radioactive, and you're the only one who's wearing a protective suit?

LARRY: Let's get down to business here. Who is it? Who is the other man, goddamnit?

64

JANE: Nick Nolte.

LARRY: If I were you, I'd lay off the sarcasm, Jane. This is neither the time nor the place.

JANE: You sound like my fifth-grade teacher, Mrs. Wiltrack.

LARRY: And you sound like you're in fifth grade. Face the music and dance, Jane. Who is it?

JANE: "Face the music and dance"? What about, "You've made your bed. Now it's time to lie in it"? Or, "It's time to pay the piper."

LARRY: It *is* time to pay the piper, whoever that is. So who is the other guy?

JANE: I'm not kidding. It's Nick Nolte.

(The waiter arrives, overhearing this. He removes the empty plates, replacing them with the entrees.)

WAITER: He hasn't looked good since *Rich Man, Poor Man.* I wonder what happened. Hollywood burnout, I guess.

(He exits.)

JANE: Okay, it's not Nick Nolte. But I hear sarcasm turns him on.

LARRY: Poor guy. *(A beat.)* So, I ask you one more time. Who is it?

JANE: Just some guy.

LARRY: What do you mean, just some guy?

JANE: You don't know him.

LARRY: Where did you meet him?

JANE: Buying M and M's at a subway stop. And, no, I'm not kidding.

LARRY: You're seeing some guy you met in the subway? That's great, Jane! Do you realize what kind of diseases he could be carrying? And now I might have them. Christ, I'd be lucky if he's an old-fashioned guy and all he's carrying is that new strain of gonorrhea from Nicaragua.

JANE: What about diseases you might have? We've never really had that discussion.

LARRY: It's a little late, isn't it? After all, we've been together for six months.

JANE: Three and a half. Look, I'm not in love with this guy or anything. It's not important.

LARRY: What do you mean, it's not important?

JANE: I don't believe in sexual fidelity in the long haul, unless the outside affair interferes with the primary relationship.

LARRY: Well, obviously it is.

JANE (thinking): Maybe you're right. Maybe we're not addressing certain problems.

LARRY: Anyway, how can you call six months the "long haul"?

JANE: I don't know. I was never good at math.

LARRY: Look, let's get down to business. What did you think about the sex we had this morning?

JANE: We had sex this morning?

LARRY: I'm not so sure myself.

JANE: It was, uh, okay. You know how much I like going down on you. Really. But sometimes I feel like I should set up a Watchman on your stomach so you can watch "Dobie Gillis" reruns until you come. I mean, it takes so long that I feel like I'm making one of those funny faces that my mother always told me if I made them too often, my face would get stuck in that position. Anyway, you don't even seem interested. You never say anything while I'm doing it, you never put your hands in my hair, you just lie there like an extra in *Carnival of Souls*. To tell you the truth—

LARRY: You mean so far you've been lying?

JANE: —why do you yawn during these intimate moments? Isn't fellatio one of those areas where total honesty is bad for a relationship?

LARRY: I never yawn then.

JANE: Yes you do. You always do.

(The waiter arrives with a ten-inch grinder, applies pepper to their food, and leaves.)

LARRY: Well, I don't quite know how to say this, but I hate the way you stick your tongue in my ear when we start making out. It feels like you're looking for something.

JANE: Well, maybe your brainpan is down a quart. *(She sees Larry's annoyed reaction.)* Sorry.

LARRY: Anyway, I never yawn during any form of sex. That's all there is to it.

JANE: Yes you do. Anyway, why haven't you said anything after all these months? I always thought you liked it when I stuck my tongue into your ear.

LARRY: Sorry. I didn't want to hurt your feelings.

JANE: Couldn't you even tell me this when we took Ecstasy? I mean, I didn't even want to take it. But you talked me into it because you said *Newsweek* called it the new love drug. You said it would make us more loving. I should have been suspicious when *New York* magazine made it a cover story.

LARRY: In case you haven't realized it, you can still be covert even while under the influence of Ecstasy.

JANE: Well, I guess I did realize it, because when you asked me when we were on Ecstasy where I was that night that you didn't know, and I said I was with Judy, I was really out with that other guy. The thing about Ecstasy was, I could lie without feeling guilty about it. Maybe they should call it Agony instead, because now I don't feel so good.

LARRY: I don't know what to say. The whole thing just scares me, I guess.

JANE: What scares you?

LARRY: You and me. Do you know that even though I've been in psychoanalysis for ten years, I can't remember the last time I cried?

JANE: What are you afraid of?

(The waiter arrives, asking about dessert.)

WAITER: Elizabeth Taylor's face dropping in the middle of a fund-raiser.

LARRY *(to waiter):* Do you think you could come back in a couple of years?

WAITER *(nonplussed):* You must be getting to the boring part. If you're not too blocked, just call when you need help.

(The waiter leaves.)

LARRY: I don't know what I'm afraid of, besides waiters like that. I used to think it was you. Then I thought it was because you and my mother both wear White Shoulders. I feel like I'm trapped in Estée Lauder's garage.

JANE: You told me that last month. All perfume smells like White Shoulders to you.

LARRY: Well, you both wear the color turquoise.

JANE: Look, your mother doesn't even wear perfume. It's cologne, not that she would know the difference.

LARRY: What's this nastiness about my mother?

JANE: Well, you're going steady with her, aren't you?

LARRY: What?

JANE: How come you always wear that ring she gave you?

LARRY: It was her mother's.

JANE: I know. You told me. The day we first met, you volunteered the information that you were saving it for the girl you were planning to marry. You told me how much you wanted to have children. Why did you say that then?

LARRY: I did not say that then.

JANE: You did too. You also told me that your mother gave you the ring when you finally used up the miles in your Eurailpass.

LARRY: She did. So?

JANE: So your ex got you back, as they say.

LARRY: Look, you're not the only one who can get deep around here. You're always complaining about me not taking the sexual initiative, like I'm supposed to be Rowdy Yates or something. Well, why don't you for a change? Why don't you ask me to go down on you instead of complaining that I don't?

JANE: What?

LARRY: You heard me. I'm not Karnak. I can't guess what you want.

JANE: I'll say.

LARRY: Look, Jane, it's too late. We know too many things about each other.

JANE: Not enough, if you ask me.

LARRY: What do you mean?

JANE: Well, I'm afraid too.

LARRY: Of what?

JANE: Tainted cheese. The laundry losing a pillowcase that my grandmother gave me. Laughing at Johnny all alone for the rest of my life.

LARRY: That's a little extreme, isn't it?

JANE: I'm afraid of you dying. You promised me when we first fell in love that you'd never die. Remember?

LARRY: No. *(A beat.)* Look, I'm sorry that I can't be as articulate about my fears as you can about yours. I don't want to lose you, but I'm going to have to let you go. Maybe it's just the fear. I can't figure anything else out. That's it. It's just the fear.

JANE: Great. I'm having dinner with FDR.

LARRY: Please Jane, no more jokes. Just this once. Promise?

JANE: Promise . . . Wait. Knock knock.

LARRY *(exasperated):* Who's there?

JANE: Larry.

LARRY: Larry who?

JANE: Larry and Jane who once had fun together because they were in love.

LARRY: Let's get back to this guy you're seeing. You must not be too happy with me if you're secretly seeing someone else.

JANE: I told you. It's no big deal.

LARRY: What do you like about him?

JANE: He says "I love you."

LARRY: I thought you said you didn't love him.

JANE: I don't.

LARRY: Does he love you?

JANE: I'm not sure. But he says it. Why don't you ever say it?

LARRY: I don't know. It makes me feel trapped, I guess. Why don't you say it to me? You used to.

JANE: Well, when you began a pattern of replying by grunting, making eye contact with the nearest switch plate, and turning on the TV set, even if the only thing to watch was a PBS special starring Viveca Lindfors, I realized I hadn't tapped into a productive vein of conversation. It makes me feel too vulnerable to say it if you don't say it back. Then, when we make love, if that's what we should call it, I wonder if you love me or if you're thinking about Kim Basinger. I'm so fucking sick of hearing about her. Don't you like the way I look?

LARRY: Sure. But that doesn't mean I don't like the way she looks.

JANE: What's that supposed to mean? You imagine that you're telling her that you love her while you're banging my brains out? Or can't you get it up unless you think she's me? Not that she has any brains, anyway, so I don't think it would be possible to bang her brains out.

LARRY: What are you so jealous of? You're the one who's seeing someone else.

JANE: It doesn't mean you're supposed to think about seeing someone else. Anyway, I told you this was nothing.

LARRY: Sex with the same person more than twice is never nothing.

JANE: You're the one who's never been with anyone for longer than a year.

LARRY: But during that year, I'm always faithful. Anyway, I

just can't believe it's nothing. In fact, I forbid you to continue seeing him. If he's really nothing, you won't care.

JANE: Only if you revoke this leave of absence business.

LARRY: Deal.

JANE: I don't know.

LARRY: What?

JANE: Maybe you're right. We do need a leave of absence.

LARRY: Is this your idea of a joke?

JANE: Uh, no, I think you know that it isn't.

LARRY: But I thought you were looking for some kind of commitment here.

JANE: Are you saying that sometimes I do move like an animal?

LARRY: Well, you used to. I'm sure that with the right strokes, you could do it again.

JANE: You know, I like it when you're this attentive. It's like it was when we first met.

LARRY: You mean, when you dropped your Filofax in the dim sum at Maxi's screening and I offered you my handkerchief?

JANE: Well, sort of. *(A beat.)* Anyway, before you talk me out of this, I still say let's just give it a rest for a while. We could both use one. Between you, you and your family, and work, I'm missing my cats' formative years.

LARRY: Whoops. We lost Jane. She's being funny again.

JANE: Or maybe she just found herself. Just give me a few weeks, okay? And then we'll reassess everything.

LARRY: In the meantime, I don't want you to censor your sense of humor. But go a little easy on the guy's ears, all right? Whosever they are . . .

(The waiter arrives with their check. Larry pays and they leave.)

LARRY *(on way out):* That salmon mousse set me back a couple of paintings.

JANE: Reparations.

WAITER *(singing like Frank Sinatra):* "That's why the lady is a tramp . . ."

MAY

AND AWAY WE GO

In which Jane asks her father for a loan so
she can move to a town that has men with
names other than Larry.

In Jane's view, all men born before December 7, 1942,
are gauche. Except for her father. Although he occasionally dresses like the official representative for the
P.G.A. tour, Frank Lazarus makes suburban living seem
almost cool, if such a thing is possible. Whereas the holy
trinity of mercantilism was once corn, silk, and slaves,
today it is life, liberty, and the pursuit of happiness—a
code that Jane's father fervently endorses. A prominent
judge in Cleveland, Frank is known not only for his
relentless disdain for procedure, but also for the exces-
sive number of times that, over a career that has
spanned twenty years, he has requested lawyers to ap-

proach the bench for a conference. This is not generally to hear both sides of an evidentiary dispute, for instance, but rather to tell a joke. Often lawyers themselves jockey for a ruling so that they can be called to the bench in order to make Judge Lazarus laugh, instead of the other way around. However, the judge's jokes are usually better.

In fact, his exceedingly serious-looking den attests to his reputation as a guy who presides over a "tough room." On the wall above his Prime Minister-style desk are testimonials from wise men such as Shecky Greene, Mort Sahl, and Buddy Hackett. The bookshelves are populated by great arbiters, great golfers, and great humorists. Right now Judge Lazarus joins his fellows, reclining on his Barca Lounger and turning on the television set. Jane enters several minutes later, her eyes caught by a quaint suburban wall plaque that says TO LIFE RAFTS, with an arrow that points to the bar (interestingly enough, the first syllable of Barca Lounger, which itself is next to the bar). Jane tries to watch what her father is watching, but since she has flown here not to see the Browns play the Steelers, but really to ask for a loan, she's somewhat preoccupied.

DAD (mouthing along with Jackie Gleason): "And away we go . . ."

JANE: Dad, I need to talk to you about something.

DAD: Jeeze, he really was the greatest, don't you think?

JANE: Yeah, Dad, Jackie Gleason was the greatest.

DAD: I mean, there's nobody who did it like Jackie Gleason. Do you realize how much fun he had? "And away we go . . ." Too much!

JANE: Dad, I really need to talk to you.

DAD: We're talking.

JANE: Dad, please. As long as I can remember, whenever I needed to talk to you about something, you said okay and then you turned on Jackie Gleason.

DAD: That's not true.

JANE: Yes it is. I remember visiting you on weekends, hoping to have you to myself, but I always had to compete with the Great One for your attention.

DAD: That's why he's the Great One. When he's in the room, all you can do is listen. (Dad cracks up at this perception.)

JANE: Dad, I can't believe this. In twenty-five years, nothing has changed. I'm here, hoping for some "quality time" and—

DAD: —Hey, listen to this. He's singing. He was so talented, I can't believe it. He had more talent in his little finger—

JANE: —Which wasn't so little—

DAD: —than Johnny Carson, Frank Sinatra, and Steve Allen combined.

79

JANE: Dad, can I borrow some money?

DAD: Oh, great! I knew it. "Dear Bank . . . I am in desperate need of funds. Please bail me out. Signed, a relative."

JANE: "And away we go . . ."

DAD: Very funny. Only you have to do it like this. *(He stands up and imitates Jackie Gleason.)* "And away we go . . ."

(He cracks up again at this gesture.)

JANE: Dad, I need five thousand dollars.

DAD: Wait a second. He's doing a "Crazy Guggenheim" bit. Jeeze, those were great.

JANE: Dad, I said I need five thousand dollars.

DAD: Have you checked with everyone else?

JANE: Who's everyone else? *(no answer)* I said, who's everyone else?

DAD: Hold on. Wow. This is really too much. A "Honeymooners" reunion—they're all there! This guy was too much, I'm telling you, he was sensational.

JANE: The greatest.

DAD: Right. "Baby, you're the greatest." You got it.

JANE: Well, I don't actually.

DAD: What?

JANE: I don't have it. "It" being money. I don't have five thousand dollars and I need it.

DAD: For what?

JANE: So I can move to a town where there are no men named Larry.

DAD: Every town has a Larry—what are you talking about?

JANE: No matter what I do, I keep meeting guys named Larry. It doesn't seem to be working out, and the only thing I can think of is to move.

DAD: Well, you've got to call it the way you see it. That's what Jackie Gleason did. He was the original "My way" guy. Believe me.

JANE: I do. I don't know why, but when it comes to Jackie Gleason, I do.

(Dad takes a sip of his drink, puts it down, and imitates the Jackie Gleason golf swing. At least Jane has always thought of it as the Jackie Gleason golf swing, but maybe it's the Johnny Carson golf swing. At any rate, her male contemporaries shoot imaginary baskets as a way to change the subject.)

JANE: So, Dad. What about the loan?

DAD: You're sure you've checked with everybody else?

JANE: Yes.

DAD: And you say this five thousand dollars is so you can move to another town and meet men who aren't named Larry?

JANE: Yes.

DAD: Fill me in on this Larry situation, will you?

JANE: Not until Jackie Gleason is over because you're not listening.

DAD: I'm listening. *(He puts hands to ears.)* See? I'm listening. Don't I look like a guy who's listening?

JANE: Dad, why is it that there's this whole generation of Dads who stand in front of their TV sets and act like Jackie Gleason?

DAD: Good taste, I guess.

JANE: No. I mean it. I don't get his appeal. Explain it to me.

DAD: He loved life.

JANE: You mean he liked martinis.

DAD: No, he loved life. I mean, look at the guy. He ate too much, he drank too much, he got too much pussy—but he was the best! Remember him in *The Hustler?*

(Dad goes into a Minnesota Fats imitation and Jane's resistance is now wearing down.)

JANE: Well, yeah, I sort of see what you mean.

DAD *(excited):* Really?

JANE: Yeah, sort of.

DAD: Let me tell you something. The great one could not turn to his parents for five thousand dollars.

JANE: How do you know?

DAD: It's a fact.

JANE: Oh, come on.

DAD: No, it's one of the things that made him great.

JANE: What can I say?

DAD: A person who needs five thousand dollars will think of something.

JANE: You're right, and I just did. I need five thousand dollars for a face lift. I know it's premature, but maybe if I look a couple of years younger, I'd meet men named Steve.

DAD: Steve's a good name. So is Larry.

JANE: Dad, tell me something about men. Why is it that they're attracted to you when you're independent, and then when you become interested in them they lose interest in you, even though they wanted you to be interested in the first place?

DAD: Is that what happens?

JANE: Dad, get serious—please. I need to know.

DAD: Men are jerks. I admit it. Isn't that what women have been saying all along—that men are jerks?

JANE: Well, yes, but I've always resisted that.

DAD: Well, don't. It's true. Men are jerks.

JANE: But women permit it to happen.

DAD: Men don't need permission to be jerks. Don't flatter yourself.

(He cracks up again at his own perception.)

JANE: Does this mean that Jackie Gleason is a jerk?

DAD: Somewhere there's probably some dame who thinks he's a jerk.

JANE: But do you think he's a jerk?

DAD: Maybe—but he's a great jerk. *(mouths along again to Jackie Gleason)* "And away we go . . ."

JANE: Dad, you're sure that the Great One is great because he never could ask his parents for a loan?

DAD: Baby, you're the greatest.

JANE: Well, away I go, to sleep. Good night, Dad. This Jackie Gleason Fest has been exhausting. Maybe we can continue this talk tomorrow?

DAD: During the British Open? We can catch it together.

(He imitates that golf swing imitated by Dads everywhere.)

DAD: Good night, Jane.

JANE: Good night, Dad.

DAD: Baby, you're the greatest.

JUNE

TO WAKE UP IN THE CITY THAT NEVER SLEEPS

In which Jane follows the First Lady's advice
and just tells a fellow to take a hike,

Jane is at the opening of a new nightclub called Belle's.
Belle's is the confluence of every nouveau riche current
of the eighties. The club itself is on three levels. The
main level is an elegant drawing room as long as a
football field. People from all walks of the over
$40,000-a-year life sit here, some consuming chic
comestibles and potables, others vying for a mention in
magazines written by people who go to clubs and write
articles about who was at what club, and others just
sitting, stymied by the Magna Carta decor, as if waiting
for their parents to come in and tell them to stop playing
in the living room. At the back of the room sits Belle,

eponymous you-know-what of the ball, dressed unlike everyone else except for a gay man downstairs on the dance floor: in a tight, Storyville corset with fishnet stockings and high-heel shoes with Oldsmobile grillwork. Belle is surrounded by a small mob of latter-day gunslingers—"My money market account is ten inches; how big is yours?" Members, or people who wait long enough at the front door for sloppy seconds, are lucky because once in, they get the East Coast equivalent of parking validation in L.A. They get to see Belle's breasts.

Downstairs, there's a swirl on the dance floor. The modern gentry moves to a well-programmed mix of music from the fifties, sixties, seventies, now, the future, which for this crowd involves a subscription to a food and wine magazine (although some of them don't know it yet).

Upstairs are a bunch of famous people, many of whom work in the comedy business, several of whom are not short.

Jane steps up to the bar and gets a glass of champagne. Ordinarily drinks are ten dollars, but since tonight is the opening, they're free—and in heavy demand. A very handsome guy in a Brooks Brothers suit approaches Jane, drink in hand. He looks to be about thirty. This is Eric. Before Jane knows it, he's clinking her glass in a toast.

ERIC *(mock ladies' man style):* So. I'm a guy, you're a girl, let's fuck.

JANE: Okay.

ERIC: What?

JANE: You heard me.

ERIC: Yeah, but this is supposed to take a little longer.

JANE: Why pretend? We know what everybody's here for.

ERIC: Don't you even want to know anything about me?

JANE: I already know something about you, and what I know I like—sort of.

ERIC: Sort of?

JANE: I told you we shouldn't get into this. I'm a girl, you're a guy, so let's fuck.

ERIC: Don't you want another drink?

JANE: Okay. I'm drinking champagne.

ERIC: What kind?

JANE: The house champagne. It's not too bad.

ERIC: I'll order a bottle of Taittinger. Let's drink that first, and then fuck. Think you can wait?

JANE *(surveying Eric):* I think I can manage.

(Jane and Eric grab stools at the bar and sit down. Eric orders.)

ERIC: So, what do you do?

JANE *(been asked too many times):* I'm a tree surgeon.

ERIC *(going along with it):* Been busy lately?

JANE: There's a lot of Dutch elm disease in the suburbs. I'm on call twenty-four hours. I haven't slept in days. I saw something on "Sixty Minutes" about tree surgeon burnout, and I thought about trying to pace myself but then, who would take care of the trees?

ERIC: I know what you mean. Aren't you going to ask what I do?

JANE: What do you do?

ERIC: I buy and sell money like Mickey Rourke in *9¹/2 Weeks.*

JANE *(muttering to herself):* Why is that movie part of my life, as opposed to, say, *Top Hat? (a beat)* Anyway, it's more like *9¹/2 Minutes* if you ask me.

ERIC: I don't have that problem, so don't worry.

(A bottle of Taittinger arrives, and the bartender pours them each a drink.)

ERIC *(raising glass in toast):* Drinking well is the best revenge.

JANE: I'll drink to that. *(They toast.)* So you're one of the few Wall Streeters who wasn't arrested today. What happened?

ERIC: There's no arbitrage involved in what I do. I take risks but I don't know which way the German mark is going to move. Today, I couldn't even get up to go to the bathroom because the market was so volatile. So I had a bottle of Tums for lunch instead of a free meal with a client at Twenty-one. Anyway, the yen killed the dollar and by the end of the day it all worked out, because I made a nice pile of dough. Should be like this for a while, based on the fact that the Giants won the Super Bowl. Whenever an NFC team wins, there are more housing starts, and that's good for the market.

(A beat while Jane ponders this.)

JANE: Are you what they call a yuppie?

ERIC: That's what my mother's always asking. I tell her I make too much money to be a yuppie, plus I drive a Porsche, not a BMW.

JANE: Driving well is the best revenge?

ERIC: Something like that. Let's dance.

(They move over to the dance floor. Eric isn't exactly in the groove, even though he seems to think that he's Tina Turner as he sings along to "Private Dancer." Jane has better moves, although a bit self-conscious.)

JANE *(loudly, over music):* Do you think Tina Turner has fellatio lips?

ERIC: I'd like to find out.

JANE: So would every white boy.

ERIC *(proudly):* That's me. White boy.

(His dancing takes on a renewed frenzy. After one or two more songs, they return to the bar and resume drinking.)

ERIC: What kind of perfume are you wearing?

JANE: Paris, by Yves St. Laurent.

ERIC: Nice. I'm wearing Krizia's new cologne for men. What do you think?

JANE: The only thing I smell in here is Gitanes, courtesy of Princess Andrea von Stumm and her Eurotrash crowd.

ERIC *(leaning toward Jane):* Here. Smell.

(Jane does.)

JANE: Krizia, huh?

ERIC: Krizia. Want to fuck now?

JANE: I never thought that the word "Krizia" would unlock my chastity belt, but I don't see anything wrong with smelling the one I'm with. I guess.

ERIC: Let's go to my place.

JANE: Couldn't we go to my place? I have to feed my cats.

ERIC: Where do you live?

JANE: Midtown.

92

ERIC: Like I said, let's go to my place. It's closer. *(He gives her a kiss.)* Don't worry. Your cats will appreciate you more when you finally show up and open up those cans of Nine Lives.

JANE: Or the Mickey Rourke version—Nine and a Half Lives.

ERIC: Quick. Hope you can slow down for a while.

JANE: I'll explain to them that it was the Krizia.

(It is a little while later. Jane is sitting on the couch in Eric's apartment. The look is fashionably nondescript. In this atmosphere, the poster of Grace Jones passes as interesting. Eric returns from the kitchen with a bottle of champagne and two glasses.)

ERIC: Piper-Heidsieck. But it's very rare. A client gave a case of it to me as a bribe.

JANE: Insider effervescing?

ERIC: Very inside. *(He pours her a glass and hands it to her.)* Here. Have some effervescence.

(They toast and sip.)

ERIC: So. Tell me about yourself.

JANE: Do I have to?

ERIC: Besides this tree surgeon gig, do you have a day job?

JANE: I'm a writer.

ERIC: I knew it.

JANE: How did you know?

ERIC: Let me put it this way. I knew you weren't a photo stylist. And all the girls at that party were either photo stylists or writers.

JANE: And Belle.

ERIC: I knew you weren't Belle because you don't have to show off your breasts. They're nice—I can tell.

(They start to make out. They like it. Ineptly, Jane mentions the subject of safe sex. Ineptly, Eric reacts.)

ERIC: Why are you bringing this up now?

JANE: I couldn't think of a way to bring it up earlier, and it seemed like there wasn't much time left, so that's why I'm bringing it up now. Sorry about the timing.

ERIC: My point is, why bring it up at all?

JANE: Something to do with wanting to stay alive, I guess.

(She disentangles herself from Eric. He turns off the compact disc of Andreas Vollenweider.)

ERIC: Don't you think you're being hysterical?

JANE: No.

ERIC *(hysterically):* You're implying that I'm carrying around a deadly disease because I haven't been careful about the people I've slept with.

JANE: I don't think that's what I'm implying. What I'm saying is, no matter how careful each of us has been, we don't know how careful our partners may or may not have been.

ERIC: You're missing my point. The press makes a big deal out of AIDS because it sells papers. This is the biggest story since killer bees.

JANE: What about the attorney general? What's he selling?

ERIC: He's probably running for President.

JANE: Look, Eric, I'm not going to beg you to wear a rubber so we can have sex.

ERIC: That's good, because I don't have rubbers here anyway. Haven't worn one since eleventh grade.

JANE: Well, I'm a good Girl Scout. I'm prepared.

ERIC: Hey, look. I don't think you've gotten the message. No way am I going to wear protection. It ruins sex. I've slept with a lot of women in my life, and no one has ever asked me to put on a glove. I've never had a disease in my entire life that you can get from a fuck, so I don't see why suddenly, you think I'm carrying—

JANE: Eric, I'm going home now.

ERIC: —some kind of disease that you get in clubs called The Ramrod—

95

JANE: Eric, wake up and smell the twentieth century. I'm following Nancy Reagan's advice. I'm just saying no.

ERIC: Well, go to the head of the class. You're the one who probably knows IV drug users, you're older than I am. *(more hysterically)* Jimi, Janis, Karen Carpenter—you probably knew them all—

(Jane quickly dresses and rushes out of Eric's apartment. Eric continues to defend himself loudly. Downstairs, Jane hails a cab. A Checker screeches to a halt. Jane gets in and tells the driver where she's going.)

DRIVER *(eyeing her in rearview mirror):* What're you—a writer?

JANE *(wearily):* No, I'm a tree surgeon.

(The cab disappears into the Manhattan night, as Jane sinks into the seat.)

JULY

LUNCH #2

In which Trish and Jane meet to discuss men
and end up discussing them.*

Jane and Trish are having lunch again, at their favorite
tearoom. They haven't seen each other for a while,
because Trish has been too busy helping a client attempt
a corporate take-over via a greenmail scheme so Byzan-
tine that it would confound a monk who made vinegar
as a cover for Vatican hijinks; and Jane has been too
busy working on her next novel, which to her surprise
and enjoyment isn't about anyone she knows, although
it does include a character named Lorenzo (she couldn't
resist). The two friends eagerly exchange the news of
the day.

* Post-AIDS

JANE: So I fall in love with this guy who loves getting head but now that we're supposed to worry about safe sex, I can't go down on him because the pre-ejaculatory fluid might have the evil A-word.

TRISH: Is that irony or satire?

JANE: Honk if you know the difference.

(They click glasses and swill down the rest of the first round of kir royales, if swilling is what you do to a kir royale, which at least in Jane's case, it is.)

JANE: Anyway, what are you doing about the problem?

TRISH: What problem?

JANE: Safe sex.

TRISH: I'm just taking my chances. I screen partners carefully and if they either haven't ripped off their grandmother for a fix lately or been to Haiti in the past nine years, then I figure it might be okay to sleep with them.

JANE: Sounds like Russian roulette to me.

TRISH: What's wrong with that?

JANE: I don't believe this. You're a careful person. Your clothes are always pressed. Since when is a fuck worth dying for?

98

TRISH: I wouldn't put it that way.

JANE: I don't see how else to put it. Hey, Trish, you know me. If it interferes with lust, I'm not interested. But ever since—

TRISH: —Yeah, yeah, ever since jury duty you've begun to think much more seriously about everything. You and my mother. Listen, Jane, I know what really goes on when people are sequestered. I mean I'm a lawyer, and I thought I had heard everything when it comes to juries, but when my mother told me about shacking up with some heavy metal freak she met during a murder trial—the jury system may have its problems, but I never thought it would turn into a salad bar for civic-minded singles.

JANE: Think back, Trish. Way back before the Shearson–American Express merger. If you can remember back that far. Is it coming back to you yet—the days when being a lawyer actually meant being responsible for someone's fate?

TRISH: Okay, sorry. I'm not making fun of your jury duty experience. I know that the whole experience was very pivotal for you, that you had a moral epiphany about your American citizenship, and the idea that you were sequestered with people of many backgrounds in a colorful motel that specializes in hung juries—

JANE: —I'll say—

TRISH: —And, of course, you just happened to have a peppy soirée with the cop who was guarding the jury—

JANE: All right, all right. So I found the party at the courthouse.

TRISH: So did my mother.

JANE: If she's happy, you should be happy.

TRISH: She is and I'm not.

JANE: I'll be right back. I think my fingers are telephonically peaking. They have to dial a phone right now!

(She rushes off. Jack, the waiter who introduced himself to Trish a few months ago, approaches Trish with another round.)

JACK *(serving drinks):* So. Bernard Goetz. Guilty or innocent?

TRISH: Hey! We didn't order more drinks.

JACK: This round's on me.

TRISH: On a waiter's salary?

JACK: No, on a retired lawyer's salary. Feel better now?

TRISH *(sincerely):* I'm sorry. *(She waits for a moment, then takes a sip.)* I'm always suspicious of anything that's free, but when it comes to champagne, just call me Bubbles. *(quickly)* Did I say that?

JACK: You didn't answer my question. Bernard Goetz—yay or nay? I know you've got an opinion.

TRISH: First of all, is it Bernard or Bernhard? Do you know?

(A woman at another table signals Jack and he excuses himself.)

JACK *(calling out):* Would you defend him if he spells it with an "h"?

(Jane returns.)

JANE: Too many people calling their machines. I'll wait for the lunch crowd to get too drunk to care about their messages, and then I'll try again. Anyway, as I recall, the case is heterosexuals versus safe sex.

TRISH: I'm not against safe sex, I'm just in favor of fun albeit sensible sex.

JANE: At this point, with everything that is known about the evil A-word, I don't think that simply screening partners is the most sensible thing you could do. Believe me, Trish, I've given this a lot of thought. I'm seriously considering the idea of trying to attain sexual nirvana with one person—forever!

TRISH: Dare I say that that person walks the face of the earth bearing the name of "Larry"?

JANE *(coyly):* Whoever it is, I'm ready to settle down with him.

TRISH: That might be because you're getting, pardon the expression, older, and you're actually, excuse my adjective

101

selection, tired of having to tell your life story to a different man every six months.

JANE: Maybe, but I bet you never thought I'd become the voice of reason on the wild frontier of contempo living.

TRISH: Well, here's my bombshell. Things aren't so great between me and Robert. I don't think this relationship is it for me.

JANE: But you don't seem that upset. You don't even look upset.

TRISH: I'm not upset. That's not the bombshell. What I'm getting at is, now that everyone else is talking about settling down, even you, I'm ready to take my chances with promiscuity.

JANE: Are you serious?

TRISH: Does the Pope stand up in his car?

JANE: Trish, what's gotten into you?

TRISH: Boredom, I guess. Claustrophobia. Whenever I'm with Robert these days, I feel like checking into an oxygen tent.

JANE: You're not going to freak out and develop an addiction to Jolt Cola, are you?

TRISH: I don't know. I never thought I'd say this, but for once maybe you're more sensible than I am. Exactly what are you doing that's so sensible?

JANE: Well, first of all, I carry around a rubber at all times. *(noticing drinks)* Hey, you ordered another round already?

TRISH: No, Jack did.

JANE: Jack?

TRISH *(indicating waiter):* Jack.

JANE *(impressed):* Heterosexual.

TRISH: It won't last. Even Rambo would lose it after serving twenty thousand orders of grilled radicchio.

JANE: If I didn't feel like a guy before, I do now.

TRISH: Did you actually buy the rubbers yourself?

JANE: I'm afraid I did. Doing it the first time was the most embarrassing thing I've done since asking for super Tampax . . . last week.

TRISH: Yeah, that's one thing that never gets any easier in life.

JANE: Well, asking for rubbers probably won't either. Actually I should start trying to say "condoms," because that's what you say when you ask for them in stores. You march right up, take a deep breath, of course making sure to wear shades so you don't have to make eye contact with the guy at the cash register, and somehow try to say, as if you've been saying it all your life, like it's asking for a package of Trident, which I think is made out of the same materials, "Excuse me, where are the condoms?"

TRISH: Maybe this whole thing vindicates Jan Morris. The only women who won't have a problem at the point-of-condom-purchase are the ones who were men first.

JANE: Anyway, that's what I've been doing—buying my own condoms. The other day I was in a store buying some and this woman in line behind me overheard me saying, "Excuse me, where are the condoms?" and she slapped me on the shoulder and said—I mean, boomed—"I'm so glad you asked that. I was wondering too, but I didn't have the nerve to ask. Good for you!" There I was, relieved at having gotten through the horror of my request, and then some woman—women and their big mouths!—has to issue a goddamn award. Can't women keep anything to themselves?

(A beat.)

TRISH: It's sad, isn't it?

JANE: What's sad?

TRISH: Everything.

JANE: Trish, are you drunk?

TRISH: No, but I wish I were. Where's that next round?

(She motions to the waiter, and it arrives. They start sipping.)

JANE: Well, I know what you mean. The other day I was stripping my bed so I could take my sheets to the Fluff and Fold and I started thinking, "Gee, my sheets may never have come stains again. They're ancient history." And I started to cry.

TRISH: Yeah, but you cry when Tom Brokaw signs off.

JANE: I know, but this is really sad.

(They sip again, saying nothing.)

TRISH: You know, if you can't exchange bodily fluids, what's the use?

(They sip again.)

JANE: And if you've got to make the person you love cover himself up with a Hefty bag, why bother?

(They sip again.)

TRISH: And if you've got to assume that you're both dying before you even start living . . .

(Now they both burst into tears and share a moment of hysterical crying. But suddenly their food arrives, and they become self-concious about the ovarian nature of their behavior, and stop crying. They start eating, and then resume the conversation.)

TRISH: So what kind of rubbers, I mean condoms, do you use?

JANE: Well, first I started carrying around the ever-popular Trojans, because it's the one that seems to be in all of the stores, and it was less embarrassing to ask for than "The

Conqueror." But then this guy I know said that wearing a Trojan is like putting on a wet sock. So then I consulted my hairdresser, figuring that he'd know what men like, and he suggested some state-of-the-art Japanese brand, which according to him is "the next best thing to skin," which I now use.

TRISH: What do men say about them?

JANE: Well, I'm no expert—

TRISH: You mean, you're no angel.

JANE: No, that's Gregg Allman. Anyway, maybe I have been doing a little "hands-on" research. And, like I said, guys don't seem to mind those Japanese condoms.

TRISH: But they're not wild about them.

JANE: Would you be wild about not being able to feel any sensation in the most sensitive part of your body during the most sensational act that men and women are capable of?

TRISH: Sounds like normal sex to me. I haven't had a sensation down there in centuries . . .

JANE: Oh, come on.

TRISH: I'd like to.

JANE: Hey, you're starting to sound like a magazine article.

TRISH: Maybe it's my turn to be sexually peaking.

JANE: Well, like I've been saying, all the more reason to

practice safe sex. Of course, heterosexual men don't seem to take the situation very seriously. They seem to think that it's basically an issue that involves fags and skin poppers or skin-popping fags and that they're so virile, they could fend off the penetration of the biggest, the most relentless, the most throbbing virus.

TRISH: What you're saying is they're not about to volunteer to wear a condom, unlike in high school.

JANE: Right. Now, it's sort of like when we were in college and they expected us to be on the pill. We thought it was so liberating—

TRISH: —And it was—

JANE: —Yeah, but it also meant that there was one more thing that men didn't have to take responsibility for—their sperm. It makes perfect sense. They can never find anything else. Their underwear, their car keys, their wallets, it's all the same. We find everything for them. With the pill, they didn't even have to worry about spilled reproductive juices. We took care of it for them. And now they expect us to do it again by carrying around condoms.

TRISH: Well, I guess somebody's got to carry around a condom. Even if I don't, I'm glad that you do.

JANE: I know, but it doesn't seem to be meeting with a good response. It's like something a man should do, but since he doesn't, we have to, but then when we tell them about it, they get upset.

TRISH: How do you mean?

JANE: Well, the other night, I was out with this investment banker, someone who managed to survive sweeps week on Wall Street, although, the way he was talking, I wonder if he isn't some kind of yuppified carnival barker.

TRISH: Would that upset you?

JANE: No, because I don't think I'll be seeing him again. After a relatively interesting evening of flirting, we went back to his apartment, where after we exchanged a modicum of information—he about the political situation at Goldman Sachs, me about how the only thing I know about bonds is the social studies bond I won in sixth grade—we start making out, and it was pretty intense, and I stop him and bring up the subject of—

TRISH: Safe sex.

JANE: Right.

TRISH: That sounds like really bad timing.

JANE: It was. But I didn't know when else to bring it up. I mean is there a good time? Can you discuss it during dinner after your first drink? "Well, now that we've both loosened up a bit, I've got something to ask. Assuming that later tonight, after we've both given the matter some thought and assessed each other's jewelry, credit rating, and table-getting ability at after-hours clubs, we'll probably, uh, *fuck,* so would you be willing to cover your unit with a protective rubber sock? You can take your pick. I just happen to have several varieties—Protex? Oh, you don't like those? How about this new kind from Japan? You know what they say— 'No glove, no love.' ''

TRISH: See—that's why I don't bother.

JANE: Neither did Liberace.

TRISH: We don't know that for a fact.

JANE: Anyway, the point is, there is no such thing as good timing when it comes to this particular discussion. Believe me, I know. Of course, I admit that to bring it up during a heated session of heavy petting was probably a bad move.

TRISH: So what happened?

JANE: He went bonkers. He said I was accusing him of having a disease, and he was positive that all of the other women he had ever slept with were carriers of nothing, except various demands, evidently, otherwise why wasn't he with any of them? And then—are you ready for this?—at the end of this bizarre tirade about his health, he says, ''Your hairdresser is probably a fag and I bet you slept with him once. All women are in love with their hairdressers!''

TRISH: *Have* you ever slept with Shugi?

JANE: Trish!

TRISH: Just kidding. Anyway, it sounds like this guy went bonkers. Maybe he didn't know how to use a rubber, I mean condom.

JANE: Yeah, maybe, and I scared him.

TRISH: Or maybe he just figured, "It can't happen to me. I'm an investment banker at Goldman Sachs."

JANE: Maybe.

TRISH: Well, there must be a way to make the safe sex encounter an exciting one.

JANE: I wish I knew what it was.

TRISH: Let's put on our thinking caps and give this sixty seconds.

(Jane gives Trish a look. They start laughing.)

JANE: Five minutes.

TRISH: Five minutes.

(They order more kir royales and think silently as they sip.)

TRISH: Dare I say "Eureka"?

JANE *(excitedly):* You've got the answer?

TRISH: I believe I do. From now on, at the moment of entry you lie back, desperately craving the hot meat injection, and say in your deepest, sexiest, most animal-like voice, as if it's the one thing you've been waiting for since you first got wet inside, "Honey, please, don't forget this. Condoms turn me on. Whenever a guy wears one, I lose control."

(Jane gives Trish the high-five on this, then gets up from the table.)

JANE: I'll be right back.

TRISH: Does the telephone have anything to do with this?

(But Jane is gone before Trish finishes the question. Jack approaches.)

JACK: It always does.

TRISH: Counselor, this is entirely out of order.

JACK *(pleased):* Thank you.

TRISH: I can't exactly say that you're welcome.

JACK: Neither could the judge. Any judge. Which is why I'm here and not in court. Which reminds me—you haven't answered my question. Bernard Goetz—what do you think?

TRISH: I think he was achin' for a breakin'.

JACK: But would you have defended him?

TRISH: I will defend anyone who can afford me.

JACK: So, I'm right. You are a hired gun.

TRISH: Let me ask you a question. If Bernard Goetz came here for lunch, would you wait on him?

JACK *(responding to someone at another table):* Excuse me, I'll be right back.

(He leaves. Jane returns.)

JANE *(referring to waiter):* Do you think he practices safe sex?

TRISH: Probably not.

JANE: I haven't seen Larry since I've adopted the policy.

TRISH: Is that why you keep calling him?

JANE: If I'm calling Larry, how do you know which one it is?

TRISH: Does it matter? *(Jane gives her a look.)* Just kidding.

JANE: If I start seeing him again, how can I bring it up without offending him, since we've already spent at least twelve weekends and a car trip together practicing unsafe sex?

TRISH: It's tricky. Maybe he'll bring it up.

JANE: Right. Newsflash: Rubbers turn *him* on.

TRISH: Well, you never know.

JANE: Anyway, I'm having fun dating these days, so I don't really care what Larry thinks.

TRISH: Somehow, I don't quite believe that.

JANE: No, you don't understand. I'm finally at the age where I feel comfortable being a girl. I don't have to pretend that I'm not one. All those years when I refused to wear pink . . . all that time I spent not dating.

TRISH: Jane, you haven't not dated since third grade. What are you talking about? You're the one person I know who always has a boyfriend.

JANE: I am?

TRISH: You are.

JANE: Well, I guess it seems more fun now. I don't know why. It just does.

TRISH: Even with condoms?

JANE: Oh, those. I forgot for a minute.

TRISH *(raising glass in toast):* Here's to *those.*

JANE *(toasting):* To those.

(A beat.)

Well, I guess since you've been with Robert all this time, you don't have to worry, anyway. I'm sorry if I've been hectoring you. I wouldn't want to sound like the "Our Miss Brooks" of passion.

TRISH: Jane, one thing you will never sound like is the "Our Miss Brooks" of anything.

JANE: Good, then I'll reiterate. If you do happen to have the occasion to use a condom, for instance with a new partner, might I suggest that you suggest that he wrap that little frankfurter in a blanket.

TRISH: Message received.

JANE: And you know what to say.

TRISH: "It turns me on."

(They laugh and toast again, but then stop laughing. In fact, Trish seems very lugubrious and Jane is strangely silent. Jack notices the silence as he heads for a neighboring table.)

TRISH: Should we be laughing at this?

JACK *(interrupting loudly):* You know what they say. Laugh and the world laughs with you. Sue and you sue alone.

JANE: Should we be laughing at that?

TRISH: I don't know. I'm afraid to flag him for the check because if he has a legitimate excuse to come over here, he's going to make me discuss Bernard Goetz.

JANE: Well, he is awfully major-mondo looking. If you don't want to discuss Bernard Goetz, I believe I could hold forth for a good ten, maybe fifteen minutes.

TRISH: Jane, I thought you only got interested in men named Larry.

JANE: Maybe it's time to cast off and try uncharted seas.

TRISH: You just did that, remember?

JANE: If Columbus had headed back to Spain after the first storm, he never would have discovered America. Then, there would be one more day that banks are open Wouldn't that be awful?

114

TRISH *(motioning to Jack):* Check, please.

JANE: Look, Trish, I was just kidding about Jack. I'm not interested, really. You can have him. I mean it. But maybe you could ask him if he has any friends. As long as they're not named Larry.

TRISH: Jane, my mission in life is not to procure escorts for you, especially if it means missing out on a potential escort myself.

JANE: Then you are interested?

TRISH *(noticing Jack approaching):* Jane, don't you have a phone call to make?

JANE *(worried):* He's not there.

(Jack brings the check.)

JACK *(to Trish):* If you'd like to continue this Bernard Goetz discussion, here's my number.

(He hands her a piece of paper. Trish awkwardly puts it away as Jack leaves. Jane toasts Trish.)

JANE: Promise to keep me posted?

TRISH *(annoyed):* There's not going to be anything to post.

JANE: Just remember to say, "Condoms turn me on."

TRISH: Not to mention champagne.

(They clink glasses again and drink up.)

AUGUST

NOT ON THE THIRD DATE

In which Trish also follows the First Lady's
advice and just tells a fellow to take a hike—
to the other side of the room.

Trish and her longtime beau, Robert, have recently
joined the list of couples who were together only because it "seemed like a good idea at the time." A pro-
duction executive in the New York office of a major
movie studio (translation: When presented with a movie
idea, he could say "no," but he couldn't say "yes"),
Robert was offered the same job with slightly higher
pay, his own parking space, and a leased foreign car in
Los Angeles. He couldn't turn it down. He and Trish
resolved to continue their relationship over the phone,
and once a month in person. But Robert couldn't come
to New York last month because he had to have an

emergency meeting with Chuck Norris about a new project called *Attack of the Ninja Nuns,* and Trish couldn't come to Los Angeles because she had to prepare for a preliminary hearing on the Ivan Boesky-Wall Street-insider-trading-the-dice-are-loaded-and-the-dealer-works-for-the-house case that was the basis for every dinner party conversation in Manhattan one week. Trish and Robert hadn't been getting along so well anyway, ever since Robert started hanging around with certain people in the movie industry who had no discernible point of view about anything but nevertheless felt compelled to express themselves by either writing, directing, or producing. Things really got bad the day Robert said, "You know, I really respect writers. Some of them are really crazy, but if they have to throw up first to get to the genius, then I'm all for it." It didn't help that he said this in front of Jane.

Trish has just returned to her apartment with Chris, an advertising consultant, who over the years has been responsible for such slogans as "Chill out with wine coolers" and "Buy an I.R.A. and a Chevrolet." Right now, he and Trish are at a crucial moment in their interspecies communication: the treacherous waters of the third date.

TRISH *(calling from kitchen):* Would you like something to drink?

CHRIS: Do you have any beer?

TRISH: No. Just various forms of water—like tea, coffee, or water.

CHRIS *(joking):* Generally, I don't have water at this hour—I just can't shake hangovers like I used to. But I can't let you drink alone.

(Trish starts singing the George Thorogood song, "I Drink Alone." The lyrics are drowned out by the sound of running water. An awkward moment passes.)

TRISH *(calling over running water):* Sorry. I'm waiting for the water to run clear. As soon as I win my next case, I'm planning to buy myself a water filter.

CHRIS: What?

(Trish turns off the water, brings two full glasses into the living room and puts them on the coffee table.)

TRISH: I'd offer you something to eat, but the only thing I have in the icebox is—

CHRIS: Don't tell me. Ice cubes?

TRISH: You got it.

(They both laugh.)

CHRIS: Sounds like my fridge. Only the ice isn't really in cubes, it's in slabs.

TRISH: Somebody once said that if there's one thing everybody could use, it's a wife. *(stage whisper)* Why did I say that? I was just trying to be witty, and I stupidly used the word "wife."

CHRIS *(protesting a little too much):* Not that I'm looking, but where do you find these "wives"? *(stage whisper)* Why did I have to say, "Not that I'm looking"? I was just trying to sound charmingly male, and now she'll think that I'm ready to be reeled in. Well, good luck, sister!

TRISH: Well, it's not like there's a P.O. Box or anything. Anyone can be trained for wifery and do things like shop for canned goods. Even you, for instance. *(stage whisper)* That should throw him off.

CHRIS: Nah, I'm completely untrainable. Whenever I go into a grocery store, I get lost in the beer aisle. You, on the other hand, I bet you've zeroed in on some canned goods in your time. *(stage whisper)* That should throw her off.

TRISH *(throwing up her arms in mock confusion):* Okay, I admit it. I can find the tuna packed in water with a blindfold on, but to tell you the truth, I don't know where anything else is.

CHRIS: What about Progresso white clam sauce—I bet you could zone in on that stuff faster than a Yugoslavian on a pair of stone-washed jeans.

TRISH: How do you know about that? I thought the only brand name you knew was Budweiser.

CHRIS: My last girlfriend loved Progresso white clam sauce. Not red, *white.* It was her favorite canned good. When Hurricane whoever-it-was was supposed to hit, she was the only person in her high-rise who didn't tape up her windows. Too busy stocking up on Progresso.

TRISH: Did you break up because you got tired of having spaghetti with the same sauce?

CHRIS: Trish, did you say "spaghetti"?

TRISH *(baffled):* Uh, yeah, I said "spaghetti." Is that okay?

CHRIS: This could be serious.

TRISH: What?

CHRIS: I mean it. This could be serious.

TRISH: Chris, what are you talking about?

CHRIS: Nancy always called spaghetti "pasta." I hated that. You called spaghetti "spaghetti."

TRISH: Uh, thanks, I guess.

CHRIS: I mean, anything that you put canned clam sauce on top of, it's spaghetti, right?

TRISH: That's why you broke up—because she called spaghetti "pasta"?

CHRIS: Nah—I mean yes. Well, no, that sounds awful. We broke up because she wanted a commitment and I couldn't give her one.

TRISH: Ah, that attractive state of being: wanting a commitment. It's like having bad breath and no matter how much Lavoris you use, it won't go away.

CHRIS: Why do you say that? Everybody has needs. It could have been me wanting the commitment.

TRISH: Usually when you hear about couples breaking up over commitment problems, it's the guy who won't make one.

CHRIS: That's not necessarily true. You just think it is because girls are on the phone more often than guys are, talking about what creeps men are and how they won't make commitments. Men think all the same things, but instead of phoning their friends to complain, they spend time making a lot of meaningless decisions.

TRISH: Maybe. Anyway, what really happened with your ex-girlfriend? Besides her linguistic gaffe?

CHRIS: She just wasn't right for me. I used to get mad at little things.

TRISH: Evidently.

CHRIS: No, come on. Listen to me. I know it sounds awful, but there were just all these little things that bugged me.

TRISH: Like what?

CHRIS: She didn't know who Roberto Clemente was.

TRISH: Roberto who?

CHRIS: He played for the Pittsburgh—

TRISH *(not really interested):* —Pirates. I know. Died in a plane crash.

CHRIS: You know about that?

TRISH: Yeah. My bestfriend is bonkers about baseball.

CHRIS: What about you?

TRISH: Well, I once drank a Pabst, but I don't know you well enough to discuss my thoughts on the designated hitter rule. Anything else?

CHRIS: Well, she liked Lionel Richie.

TRISH: So do about a billion other people.

CHRIS *(imitating him):* "Say you, say what?"

TRISH: And?

CHRIS: Well, she always had to watch wrestling. She had this weird obsession with Rowdy Roddy Piper.

TRISH: So?

CHRIS: So, I don't know.

TRISH *(half-seriously):* Hey listen, maybe we should hold everything right here.

CHRIS: What do you mean?

TRISH: If we really get involved, you might dump me when you find out that every week I drop everything so I can watch "L.A. Law," no matter what I'm doing.

CHRIS: You do? That's one of my favorite shows!

TRISH: Oh, come on. You're making that up. Someday you'll be telling someone else that you just can't explain it, you know it sounds awful, but you stopped seeing me because I had this weird obsession with the guy who plays Sifuentes.

CHRIS: No, I won't. I promise!

TRISH: I don't know. I mean you don't exactly sound like the poster child for the World Toleration Program.

CHRIS: Look, Trish, what I was trying to say was that if something had clicked, if I'd loved Nancy, I wouldn't have cared if she'd been president of the Lionel Richie fan club.

TRISH: You're sure?

CHRIS: Well, maybe that would have been pushing it, but you know what I mean.

TRISH: Yeah, I do. I mean, I still can't figure out why I broke up with the guy I was with two boyfriends ago. The only thing I can pin it on was that he performed this really awful conceptual art.

CHRIS: What was so bad about it?

TRISH: It was worse than Daryl Hannah doing that fire dance in *Legal Eagles.* Worse than Laurie Anderson in a

Day-Glo body stocking. Worse than any performance that involves folding chairs.

CHRIS: Come on. What did he do?

TRISH: He sat at a table on a bare stage for two hours and talked about not being able to find Kuwait on a map with a recording of Ethel Merman singing "Zing went the strings of my heart" coming out of a stuffed toucan and a photograph of Jimmy Hoffa on the ceiling.

CHRIS: Sounds like Spalding Gray.

TRISH: Close. He lived next door to Spalding and they both used to tap off a neighbor's gas line. Once they discovered that, they started stealing each other's ideas. Then Spalding was discovered by public television and as far as I know, Chuck is still tapping off his neighbor's gas line.

CHRIS: You ran out on a guy because he couldn't pay his Con Ed bill? And to think I had you pegged for Mother Teresa . . .

TRISH: Hey, he was just boring, that's all. That whole performance art scene, they're like charming dinner party guests who won't stop talking. Even during dessert, they're going, "When I first heard my parents make love, I was watching 'Kukla, Fran and Ollie,' and my brother was throwing a slinky down the living room stairs." The trouble with Chuck was he just never stopped trying to connect things.

(A beat. Chris isn't quite sure what to make of this.)

125

CHRIS: Well, at least you're available.

(A beat. Trish isn't quite sure what to make of this.)

TRISH *(fumbling for something to say):* Well, now that we've been beyond the valley of the exes, I guess we could discuss something more profound, like, uh, international terrorism.

CHRIS *(blurting it out):* Trish, look. I just don't know how much longer I can wait to make love with you. Jeeze—did I say that?

TRISH: Keep talking.

CHRIS: We've only seen each other twice, not counting tonight, and I can't stop thinking about you.

TRISH: I feel the same way. I mean, I just wanted to spend some time playing the field, as they say, but every time I turn my TV on and see that surfboard commercial, I picture you at your desk, scribbling away. "If it swells, ride it"?—Did you think of that?

CHRIS *(slightly embarrassed):* Actually, I did.

TRISH: It's sexy.

(A beat.)

CHRIS: So are you.

(He leans over to kiss her. She turns away.)

TRISH: I don't know, Chris. I guess I'm just a little worried.

CHRIS: I bet I know why. *(checking his watch and imitating TV announcer)* Okay, kids, what time is it? That's right. It's time for everybody's favorite topic. Health! I see we've got an eager-looking audience volunteer here, so let's get right to it, shall we? Do you—

TRISH *(wanting to get this over with):* —have a venereal disease? No. Do you?

CHRIS *(also quickly, now as himself):* Me? No. Have you ever spent time in Haiti?

TRISH: No. Have you ever slept with a man?

CHRIS: No.

TRISH: You're sure?

CHRIS: Yes, I'm sure.

TRISH: It's okay. You can tell me. I won't be offended. Every man has had at least one homosexual experience, and I think they should talk about it.

CHRIS: Is that what you read in women's magazines?

TRISH: No! Well . . . sort of.

CHRIS: Look, Trish, I've fantasized about sleeping with men but I never actually had the nerve to do it. I mean, what if he never called me back? Just kidding.

TRISH: I know what you mean. At Barnard, which was a breeding ground for baby dykelets, I used to fantasize about it myself. I even made out with one of my roommates once. That was when men were the political enemy, so it seemed like the right thing to do.

CHRIS: How was it?

TRISH: Well, like my best friend Jane says, I don't want to make out with women. Their backs are too small.

CHRIS: Okay! Let's return to the subject of health! Have you slept with a lot of guys?

TRISH *(defensively):* What do you mean by a lot?

CHRIS: More than a few and less than a great deal?

TRISH: Hmm. If I said yes would you be turned off because promiscuity translates into, "She probably has some kind of disease, but she doesn't know about it yet," or turned on because promiscuity translates into, "She probably knows the trick of the seven knots and can't wait to show it to me"?

CHRIS: I don't know. I think I'm turned on already. Otherwise we wouldn't even be having this discussion.

TRISH: Well, how about you? I mean, aside from fantasizing about but not actually sleeping with men, what else haven't you done?

CHRIS: Not very many things.

TRISH: You mean *you've* slept with a lot of girls?

128

CHRIS: Uh, yes. *(then quickly to deflect attention)* Does your dentist wear rubber gloves?

TRISH: Uh, yes. Does yours?

CHRIS: Yes. How many times have you been in a hot tub?

TRISH: A public hot tub? Never!

CHRIS: No—any hot tub. The heat breeds a lot of germs, in spite of all of those chemicals.

TRISH: Hey, what is this—the bacteria gestapo?

CHRIS: I'm sorry. It's just that once the health discussion starts, there's no end. Anyway, a guy just can't be too careful these days.

(He leans over to kiss her.)

TRISH: Neither can a girl.

(They kiss at length.)

TRISH *(breaking it off too soon):* Should we be doing this?

CHRIS: We just did.

TRISH: We barely know each other.

CHRIS: But we just had an intimate conversation.

TRISH: I know. I generally don't present a health readout on the third date.

CHRIS: Me neither. The whole thing is kind of awkward

. . . So, now that each of us has denied having a sexually transmittable disease, I think maybe it's time to test these claims . . .

TRISH: I don't know, Chris. That's not all there is to it.

CHRIS: In an earlier decade, I'd have known what to say next. If we were having this conversation in the fifties, I'd say, "Look, baby. They may drop the bomb tomorrow, and then we'd never know what it was like to experience each other . . ."

TRISH: And I'd invite you into my fallout shelter. *(stage whisper)* Of course, if I were alone in a fallout shelter, I'd probably invite any guy in.

(The lights go out and then come up again on Trish's fantasy. She is in a fallout shelter with Jane. It's stocked with row after row of Tab, tuna packed in water, and Sara Lee pineapple cheesecake. They are playing cards.)

JANE *(holding up hand and looking at it):* Got any sevens?

TRISH: Go fish.

(There is a knock at the door.)

JANE: Who is it?

FEMALE VOICE: Got anything to eat?

TRISH: Another girl.

JANE *(to voice):* Sorry. We're down to our last Tab.

(Jane and Trish look at each other and shrug: What can we do?)

TRISH *(to Jane):* Got any threes?

JANE: Go fish.

(There is another knock at the door.)

TRISH: Who is it?

MALE VOICE: Got anything to eat?

(Jane and Trish rush over to the door, open it, and a guy tumbles in. It turns out to be Chris, dressed like Mad Max in Road Warrior.*)*

TRISH: Jeeze! I thought you were dead!

CHRIS: No, just hungry!

JANE: Have a Tab!

TRISH: And some tuna packed in water! We just ran out of crackers.

(Chris wolfs down some food, and then, energized, he stands up macho-style.)

CHRIS *(like Brando):* Stella!

(The lights go out and come up again on Trish and Chris as before. Trish looks a bit distracted.)

CHRIS: And I suppose if this were the sixties, we would have met at a rock festival, and the music would have made us feel like making love in the mud—

TRISH: —even though we would only have known each other's first names.

(The lights go out and come up on a pup tent. Inside it are several hard-core flower children. A few are smoking from a bong. Jane and Trish are happily huddled under a towel, trying to dry off.)

TRISH: Did you ever think that you would stand outside in the rain for five hours just so you could see some guys who need a haircut play loud music?

JANE: Not without mascara.

(A virile-looking hippie stumbles in. He looks like Samson, but it's Chris. The hippie surveys the action in the tent.)

HIPPIE (to Jane and Trish): More foxy chicks! All right!

(He starts grooving to the music. Jane and Trish join in. The lights fade out on Jane as the hippie begins to speak.)

HIPPIE: Hi. I'm Chris from Portland. Did we know each other in a previous life?

TRISH: Let's find out.

(She grabs him and they begin to dance close. The lights fade out on them and come back up on Jane.)

132

JANE *(to audience):* Did she say that?

(The lights fade out on Jane and then come up again on Trish and Chris as before, in Trish's apartment. Trish is again a bit distracted.)

CHRIS: Well, I'm sure glad that we didn't meet in the seventies, when it might have been at a self-actualization workshop—

TRISH: —and we both would have made a point of verbalizing our needs so we could assert ourselves in bed.

(The lights fade out and then come up on Jane, Trish, Chris, and a few other men and women sitting in a circle in a classroom.)

MAN #1: I sympathize completely with women. When my girlfriend gets her period, I have cramps.

MAN #2 *(seriously):* Take heavy doses of B_{12}.

WOMAN #1: We don't need sympathy, we need space. You're not giving us any room to be ourselves.

JANE: If I want a guy who gets cramps, I'll go out with Rock Hudson.

ALL MEN: He's dead.

JANE: No, he's not. It's the seventies.

ALL MEN: Oh.

CHRIS: All I know is, I've never gotten a single cramp in my entire life.

TRISH: I didn't get your name.

(The lights go down on everybody except Jane and Trish.)

JANE: Trish, that was very brazen. How come you're not like that in real life?

TRISH: It's unseemly.

JANE: Are you saying that I'm unseemly?

TRISH: Yes.

(The lights fade out and come up on Chris and Trish as before, in Trish's apartment.)

CHRIS: Well, this is the eighties and I don't know what to say next. Do you?

TRISH: I guess I'm just trying to do what women did before people had "relationships." Take things a little more slowly. Have an actual courtship.

CHRIS: Well, I guess we've sort of been having a courtship. I've been calling you, you've called me, we've actually been dating.

TRISH: It's true. I thought I had forgotten how to date, but I guess that's what we've been doing.

CHRIS: Come on, admit it. Wasn't our first date the best first date you've ever had?

134

TRISH *(coyly):* Second-best.

CHRIS: How could you have more fun than dancing in a parking lot next to my car with the radio playing "Rock Around the Clock"? That's impossible!

TRISH: Yeah, maybe you're right. What makes you so sure of yourself?

CHRIS: Would you like me if I weren't?

TRISH: I don't know.

CHRIS: Are you sure?

TRISH: Yes . . . I mean, I don't know.

CHRIS: Look, Trish, I don't know exactly what you're trying to get me to say, but I've already promised, if you want to be true to "L.A. Law," it's okay with me. *(provocatively)* Does that mean we can relate on a physical plane now?

TRISH: I don't know. Do you think we're in love?

CHRIS: Well, when I think about you, I go weak in all the areas that you're supposed to go weak in.

TRISH: Me too. But I can't stop worrying about one thing.

CHRIS: What's that?

TRISH *(parodying a classic song):* "Will you still phone me tomorrow?"

135

CHRIS: Why does it always have to get down to a phone call? What did women do before the phone was invented?

TRISH: Except in rare instances, there was no premarital sex before the phone was invented.

CHRIS *(becoming defensive at the use of the word "premarital"):* So now you're asking for a morning-after phone call *and* a proposal?

TRISH *(becoming defensive in turn):* You know, guys are really strange. Jane is right. A girl expresses a fear, and the next thing you know, they think you're figuring out what to name the baby. You've been asking *me* out, remember?

CHRIS: And you've been responding. *(A beat)* Anyway, I've got an idea. How about if I do spend the night here, but all we do is literally sleep together? That's courtship, isn't it?

TRISH: You mean, we actually sleep together in the same bed, but we agree not to touch each other?

CHRIS: Well, maybe we could hold hands or hug.

TRISH *(sarcastically):* But wouldn't that be too much of a commitment?

CHRIS: Oh, come on. If two people can't spend some time together horizontally and stare at the ceiling and talk about their hopes and dreams, then what's the use?

TRISH: Do you steal the blankets?

CHRIS: Why don't you try me?

TRISH: Okay, but only on one condition.

CHRIS: What's that?

TRISH: We make love on our fourth date and you promise to phone me and you really mean it.

CHRIS *(laughing):* I get the feeling your terms are non-negotiable, but it's a deal anyway. *(He checks his watch.)* It's eleven forty-five. I think our fourth date should be tomorrow. What are you doing in fifteen minutes?

TRISH: I think I'll be right here next to you, wanting you to bang my brains out but wondering how to get you to wear a condom without ruining the evening.

CHRIS: I was wondering the same thing.

TRISH: You mean I don't have to lie and say, "Condoms turn me on"?

CHRIS: Do you know how many times I've heard that line? Anyway, it's the late twentieth century. When it comes to sex, we have to tell the truth—sort of. But we can still lie like crazy about everything else.

TRISH: Good. Then let's unfold this futon and fall in love.

CHRIS: No lie?

TRISH: Ask me again in fifteen minutes.

SEPTEMBER

HEY, BABY

In which several modern men bond in a new male ritual, the baby shower.

We are inside the living room of a fashionable New York apartment. Furnished in a tasteful mix of the traditional and the new, the apartment is strewn with pink streamers. There is a banner that says, CONGRATULATIONS, DAD. Dad is Matt, a building contractor who has made a lot of money refurbishing Manhattan fireplaces. He is also Larry's best friend from high school. A man's-man kind of guy in his mid-thirties, he nervously walks around the room, stopping periodically at a pink baby cradle to commune with the infant inside. This is three-week-old Chloe, who speaks in a sexy, grown-up, wordly-wise voice-over. Larry follows Matt around the room, stepping carefully over and around the evidence of modern sex: an Aprica stroller, a stuffed brontosaurus as big as a real baby of the same species, and a three-tiered diaper condo.

MATT: So, did you get the Moosehead?

LARRY *(here we go again):* Yes, I got the Moosehead. Even though I don't think that Moosehead is appropriate for a shower, I got it—just for you, Matt.

MATT: Well, this isn't exactly "a shower." It's my shower. Remember?

LARRY: I remember that it was my idea and I had to talk you into it.

MATT: No kidding. You think I'd think of something like a baby shower? *(to Chloe, as a completely different person)* So, Chloe, this is your first party. Good thing I'm here to supervise, with all these guys coming over, and you, you little heartbreaker—

CHLOE (VO): Why would I be interested in any of his friends? Bob is married, Pete has a permanent psychic erection, and Larry can't make a commitment.

(SFX: Intercom buzzer)

LARRY: Look proud. They're here.

MATT: Don't I always look proud? I mean, have I ever been ashamed of anything having to do with my sex life?

140

CHLOE (VO): No. Unfortunately, he seems proud of the fact that there are 276 women still waiting around for a phone call.

(Larry answers the intercom and buzzes in some guests.)

LARRY: Just relax, Matt. They've never been to a shower either.

MATT: Yeah, well, maybe there's a reason.

(There is a knock at the door. Larry calls out for the guests to enter. In walk two men, Bob and Pete. They are about the same age as Matt and Larry. Bob is married and has a child. He carries a shopping bag. Pete has been in love with many women, but not for longer than five minutes. He carries a box of cigars.)

PETE *(offering box):* Congratulations, Daddy-O.

MATT: Thanks, man.

PETE: Didn't know you had it in you.

CHLOE (VO): What are you talking about? He's had it in a lot of places.

PETE: Hey, fire up one of these stogies.

(Matt does, and so does everyone else.)

MATT: Guys, make sure to blow the smoke toward this smoking fan.

(He indicates and turns it on.)

Can't have smoke. We baby-proofed the house.

BOB: We did that too. Some chick came over and told us to cover up all the electrical outlets. Charged us three hundred bucks.

PETE: You know my friend Abby?

MATT: Nudge nudge, wink wink.

PETE *(annoyed):* Hands off, pal. You're married, in case you've already forgotten.

MATT: So is she.

PETE: Yeah, but she forgot. *(the guys enjoy this moment)* Anyway, she told me that her friend Betsy, who just got married, is taking a course in how to take care of a baby.

LARRY: Why can't she just read Dr. Spock like my mother did?

MATT: My mother didn't do any of those things and everything turned out *(strutting across the room like a rooster)* just fine.

CHLOE (VO): Cock-a-doodle-doo.

LARRY: Guys, settle down and think about this. If a woman doesn't know how to diaper a baby, what's wrong with reading a book or taking a course?

BOB: My wife didn't do either of those things. We have a live-in au pair girl from Denmark who knows how to do everything. Of course on her day off, Vicki and I take turns changing the diapers.

MATT: That's suburban of you.

BOB: Hey, it's one of the few chances I have to bond with my kid. In fact, sometimes I make Vicki let me spend Marta's entire day off in charge of child care. The whole thing is pretty amazing.

PETE: Oh, come off it, guys. A baby takes a dump, including yours, and you—

MATT: —clean it up.

LARRY: It's one of the few chances we get to find out what it's like to be a woman.

CHLOE (VO): You know something? This guy is right, although I get the feeling he's the type who gets sympathetic PMS.

(Matt takes a massive puff on his cigar, then merges into a leather chair.)

MATT: I'm in Havana. It's 1950. Everywhere you look, wall-to-wall broads.

CHLOE (VO): Calling all psychiatrists. This is not one of those times when a cigar is just a cigar.

LARRY: Well, according to baby shower protocol, it's time for attractive snacks.

MATT: If that means food and beer, let's do it. To quote Gary Gilmore.

CHLOE (VO): And Cole Porter.

(Larry heads for the kitchen. The others settle into the living room. Bob puts the shopping bag next to him, takes two presents out, and puts them on the coffee table.)

BOB *(awkwardly):* These, uh, are for you.

MATT: Uh, thanks.

BOB *(calling out):* Hey, don't bring any beer for Pops. He's already got some kind of paunch.

PETE: He can't help it. His body's a mess! He just had a baby.

(The guys crack up at this.)

CHLOE (VO): If men had babies, they'd argue over who had the longest stretch marks.

(Larry returns with a six-pack and a snack tray.)

LARRY: Yo! Beer here!
(They all grab one, and twist off the caps.)

PETE *(to Chloe):* Hey, baby, here's to you.

(They toast and swill it down.)

CHLOE (VO): Don't ever call me baby.

BOB *(checking his watch):* Excuse me, Chloe. Time to phone Sportsphone and get the score on the hockey game.

(Bob gets up and goes to make a phone call.)

MATT: It's all right. She speaks Stroh's.

LARRY: Yeah, it's her first language.

MATT: Well, I don't want my daughter to turn into Frank Gifford, but I would like her to be the kind of girl who could throw a few passes.

CHLOE (VO): Get a real life.

PETE: What about receiving passes?

MATT: Hey, what's that supposed to mean?

LARRY: He's just kidding, Matt. Chill out. I guess maybe you're not used to the idea of having two girls around the house yet.

MATT: What're you talking about? It just means I get to flirt twice as much, have two faithful admirers to hang on my every word . . . *(notices Chloe)* Sorry, Chloe, just kidding.

CHLOE (VO): It's okay. I wasn't listening.

(Bob rushes back in excitedly.)

BOB: The Islanders just scored two goals.

CHLOE (VO): "Western Hemisphere Disappears in Major Meltdown; Gretzky, Others Out for Season".

PETE: Well, guys, it looks like Chloe has raked in a nice little haul. Let's examine the goods, shall we?

(Larry reaches under his chair, retrieves a present, and puts it on the coffee table along with the other presents. The guys ad lib comments urging Matt to open the presents. Matt picks up one and reads the card.)

MATT: "To Matt. Way to go, chief. From Pete."

CHLOE (VO): Dad gets an A in reproduction. But what about Mom? What about me? And why say "Way to go" now? I might grow up to be someone embarrassing, like Jeane Kirkpatrick. What's sperm got to do with it?

(Matt opens the present. It's a tiny little dress with a lot of ruffles and lace. He doesn't know how to handle it and, slightly embarrassed, awkwardly puts it aside.)

MATT: Uh, thanks, man. I appreciate it. *(Picking up another present, reading card)*
"Dear Matt. I'm not big on shopping, so I hope you like this. Your fellow grown-up, Bob." *(Opening the present, and reading an engraved invitation.)* "This is to request the pleasure of Chloe Vincent's company for lunch on her sixteenth birthday at Spago."

BOB: With your permission, of course.

CHLOE (VO): Isn't that a violation of the Mann Act?

MATT: Uh, you want a date with my daughter?

BOB: Well, uh, I didn't mean it that way.

MATT *(smiling):* That's okay, pal. I'm just yankin' your crank. Just don't try and pull any fast ones.

PETE: Can I come too?

CHLOE (VO): What is this—a gang lunch?

PETE: Just kidding. But I have to say any daughter of yours is going to be some kind of piece of work.

MATT: Hey, don't talk that way about my daughter. I know if she were your daughter—if you could have one, because I don't think you have the *cajones,* to tell you the truth—I'd probably say the same thing, and I used to say the same thing about other people's daughters, but now that I have a daughter, I don't like that kind of talk. *(A beat.)* On the other hand, with Elaine's figure and my looks, she probably will be some kind of piece of work, and I'm sure she'll be able to tell guys where to get off.

CHLOE (VO): Starting with you-know-who.

PETE: Open Larry's present. He's more nervous than you are.

MATT and LARRY: I'm not nervous.

(Matt picks up the last present from the table and reads the card.)

MATT: "Dear Chloe. Just to prove that your old man looks younger every day. Love, Uncle Larry."

147

(Matt opens the present. It's a framed photo.)

MATT: Me and you at high school graduation. We were a hot team, weren't we?

LARRY: We were. Remember the time we took Sandy and Linda to Squaw Rock and made out under the space blanket?

MATT: It wasn't Squaw Rock. It was Squire's Castle. And it wasn't a space blanket, it was a sleeping bag. And we didn't make out, I did. Remember?

LARRY: No, we both made out. But I admit that you got under the bra, and I only got over the sweater.

(They laugh a lot at this.)

CHLOE (VO): And I'm sure Sandy and Linda thought it was really funny when you two chuckleheads upchucked in the driveway afterward.

MATT: Remember when you left for college and I thought we'd never hang out again because you'd probably come back with a wife?

CHLOE (VO): That's rich. Till "not having my own space" do us part.

LARRY: Hey, you know me, man. Once they say yes, I say no.

MATT: Hey, that's what I used to say.

LARRY: The torch has been passed.

MATT: You'll meet the right person one of these days.

LARRY: I meet the right person every day. That's the problem.

MATT: What about Jane? She's been very good for you. You smile like a moron when you're around her.

LARRY: I do?

MATT: Yeah, you do.

LARRY: I get nervous when anything lasts longer than six months. I'm like a runner. I can't get past that wall. I think I freaked her out. She's seeing other guys.

MATT: Good girl.

CHLOE (VO): Don't call her a girl.

LARRY: Matt, I've been wondering about something. I saw this thing on the news the other day. "Eggnog for One: Enjoying the Holidays Solo." It was for singles.

MATT: You want to stay single? Eat bologna sandwiches for the rest of your life?

LARRY: I don't like bologna sandwiches. *(glancing at Chloe)* Maybe I'll just hang out and wait for little Chloe here . . .

CHLOE (VO): Hey, pal, instead of throwing showers, maybe you should take one.

149

(A beat. Matt checks his watch.)

MATT: Well, guys, thanks for the presents. This has been great.

PETE: Hey, let's keep the party going. McGuffin's, anyone?

(He gets up and heads toward the door. Bob follows.)

MATT: Lar, you can go. I'll clean up.

LARRY: You'll clean up at your shower?

MATT: Yeah, it's cool.

(Larry joins Bob and Pete at the door and they all leave, ad-libbing good-byes. Matt has a moment to himself. Suddenly Larry reappears.)

LARRY: You all right?

MATT: Never better.

(Larry starts clearing the mess off the coffee table. He picks up the dress that Pete brought for Chloe.)

MATT: Hey! Careful with that!

(Matt takes it from Larry and begins to fold it tenderly.)

LARRY: Sorry.

MATT: Well, you were right. It was a good idea to go ahead with this shower. I'm glad I thought of it.

LARRY: It was my idea.

MATT: And if you ever have the *cajones* to knock someone up and cop to it, I'll do the same for you.

LARRY: Thanks. *(A beat.)* Just don't serve beer.

MATT: I won't. I'll serve blender drinks with tiny plastic mermaids.

CHLOE (VO): Hey, where's *my* bottle? I sure could use a shot right now.

OCTOBER

SOME LIKE IT LARRY

In which Jane's ex shows up at Jane's loft
and encounters the other men in her life.

Jane is in her midtown loft, which is as big as a bowling
alley and as sparsely furnished and dimly lit. The one
area that has received the most attention is the bedroom; it is here that the windows are properly insulated.
Also, it is here that Jane is lying in bed with—well, we'll
get to that. The doorbell rings, but Jane ignores it. It rings
again and she continues to ignore it. A few minutes later
there is the fumbling of keys at the elevator lock, which
Jane doesn't hear because she is too busy making out
with—okay, okay, we're getting to that! Finally, the
door is unlocked by Larry, the Larry of *What Gary Did*.

LARRY: Hello? Anybody home?

(Singing to himself, he walks over to a record collection housed in plastic milk crates.)
"Oooh, baby, baby. Are you here in your loft, baby, baby?"
(He starts thumbing through records, setting some aside. Jane walks out of her bedroom in a sexy silk bathrobe and starts to make coffee.)

LARRY: "Come on, baby, baby. I want to get in your soft, baby, baby."

(Jane, startled, drops the cup. Larry is startled too, and comes over to Jane.)

JANE: Larry! How did you get in?

LARRY: Sorry, baby. I didn't think you were home. I just couldn't live without hearing "Wipe Out."

(He imitates the laugh at the end of "Wipe Out.")

JANE: You don't live here anymore, you know. You think you can just waltz right in—

LARRY: I didn't waltz, I shredded. You know—that new dance from Huntington Beach? *(shredding for a moment)* What do you think?

JANE: *holding up hand and snapping fingers):* Key.
(He gives it to her.)

154

LARRY: I've got dozens. You should have changed the lock after writing *What Gary Did.* You didn't think I wouldn't have a response, did you?

JANE: I wasn't really thinking about that. I just figured, let the chips fall.

LARRY *(dropping subject):* Hey, your hair looks great short. How come you never wore it like that when we were together?

JANE: I did, remember? You kept calling me Marvin Hagler.

LARRY: Who me? I don't even like Marvin Hagler.

JANE: That was the point.

LARRY: Okay, I was a jerk then. Tell it to the judge.

JANE: I did—in my book. Remember? Isn't that why you're here?

LARRY: Did you really think people wouldn't know that Gary is me—Larry?

JANE: You're not a famous person, no damage. The only really bad thing I said is that you don't like getting blowjobs, which actually is free advertising for you since most women don't like giving them.

LARRY: You haven't lost that great sense of humor.

155

JANE: Look, Larry, why don't you just take your records and get out of here. Speaking of ''Wipe Out,'' that's what this surprise visit is turning into.

(Suddenly the door flies open and in comes Larry #2, the man Jane has been dating. He is dressed in jeans and a paint-covered shirt, having just come from his studio. He carries a Carvel ice cream cake.)

LARRY #2: Surprise! *(singing)* It's Wally the Whale, the whale with the whipped cream tail . . .

JANE: Hey, hey, hey—what's going on here? I didn't see you for a month, suddenly you waltz in—

LARRY #2: I didn't waltz, I shredded. You know that new dance from Huntington Beach?

(Jane exchanges a look with Larry #1.)

JANE: Yeah, yeah, I know all about it. What's with the ice cream cake?

LARRY #2: I thought you liked it.

LARRY #1: What's he doing with a key?

JANE: Larry, Larry. Larry, Larry. *(Everyone reacts to this.)* It's a common name among baby boomer men. Most of them are handsome Jewish princes who have a good sense of humor, like the Yankees, and aren't too tall. Believe me, I've done a lot of thinking on the subject.

LARRY #2: So every guy you know named Larry gets a key to your loft?

JANE: No, just the ones I fuck. *(The Larrys react to this.)* Just kidding.

LARRY #2: Well, I've been meaning to give the key back, but you know me—I hardly ever come downtown. When we first met, I told you that one of my fears was that you weren't geographically desirable.

JANE: Yeah, yeah. Below Twenty-third Street. I know.

LARRY #1: So who is this guy?

JANE: Larry's an artist I've been dating. His work is attracting a lot of attention.

LARRY #1 (to Larry #2): Which gallery are you with?

JANE *(hastily):* Larry's in several galleries in Europe.

LARRY #1: Sounds very major.

LARRY #2: What about you? What do you do?

LARRY #1: Besides being the Gary in Jane's book, I'm one of the editors of *Rolling Stone.*

LARRY #2: Oh yeah? Used to be a good magazine.

LARRY #1: That's okay. I don't like it either. We haven't done anything interesting since the Manson interviews. But it pays the rent, and gets me into concerts.

LARRY #2: I'll bet.

LARRY #1: I've seen James Brown thirteen times.

LARRY #2: I guess it's a man's world.

(Jane exchanges a look with Larry #2 trying to stifle a giggle at Larry #1's expense. Now, a figure approaches from Jane's bedroom. This is . . .)

LARRY #3: Good morning, toots. *(looking around)* What's this—a co-op meeting?

JANE *(awkwardly):* Uh, hi there.

LARRY #1 *(amused):* Sleep well? *(extends hand)* Around these parts, they call me Larry.

(Jane can barely contain herself.)

LARRY #3: Oh yeah? Great name. *(They shake hands.)* I'm Larry too.

LARRY #2 *(possessively):* Tell me about it. *I'm* Larry too.

LARRY #3: Well, hats off to Larry.

(Larry #1 begins to laugh. Larry #2 is upset.)

LARRY #2: Is Allan Funt on the premises? Are we catching Larrys in the hilarious act of being themselves?

JANE: Guys, look. I don't know what to say. This has to be one of the strangest, if not the strangest moment in my entire life. *(The Larrys ad-lib agreement.)* Maybe all of you should leave so I can figure out what just happened.

LARRY #1: This is highly amusing but I don't know if I can take much more of it either. I'll just get my records . . .

(He walks off to retrieve them.)

LARRY #3 *(spotting cake):* Uh, what's this? *(opening it)* Can I have some? Always like to start the day with carbos.

LARRY #2 *(rushes over and closes the lid on the cake box):* That's for Jane.

(Larry #1 returns with his records.)

LARRY #1: I'm amazed. This visit to your loft is just chock full of surprises. Guess what I just found?

LARRY #2: Don't tell me. Larry Speakes? Larry Olivier? No, no. Larry Storch! Is that it?

LARRY #1 *(excited):* I found my old Temptations record. The one with the original Motown recording of "My Girl."

LARRY #2 and LARRY #3: "My Girl"?

LARRY #1: Yeah! It's my favorite song.

(He races over to the record player and puts it on. He and Larry #3 start singing along and Jane starts dancing, Motown-style, with them. Larry #2 runs out in a huff.)

JANE *(calling out):* Larry!

LARRY #1 and LARRY #3: What?

JANE: Never mind.

(Larry #1 and Larry #3 sing the lyric, "Talkin' 'bout my girl," and start laughing uncontrollably. Jane turns off the record player and shows them out. A little while later the phone rings.)

LARRY #2 (voice-over): Jane, I was hoping that you were *my* girl.

JANE *(hesitant):* I was, I mean, I, uh—

LARRY #2 (VO): There aren't any other Larrys, are there?

JANE: Uh, no, you're the only Larry.

(A beat.)

LARRY #2 (VO): I was just wondering. Talk to you later.
(Jane hears the click of the phone, sits for a moment in a trance, and voraciously consumes the entire ice cream cake.)

OCTOBER

a bit later

FINAL GAME OF THE WORLD SERIES

In which we visit the kind of diamond that
really is a girl's best friend.

Larry and Jane are at Yankee Stadium. Jane is wearing a
T-shirt that says BILLY BALL. Larry, fresh from his studio,
is spattered with paint, and could be mistaken for a
house painter. The Yankees are, of course, playing a
team which, thanks to the hyperactive Yankee owner,
consists primarily of the previous season's Yankees.
Larry and Jane enjoy an excellent view from the third
base line, seats which Larry's art dealer gave him for the
evening, as he, hoping to meet Jack Nicholson and other
highly visible people at a party afterward, chose to at-
tend the New York Knicks–Los Angeles Lakers game
instead.

Both Larry and Jane are baseball fans, although Larry (unlike other Larrys) has always despised the Yankees and Jane has always thought they were the bee's knees, the cat's pajamas, the greatest thing since sliced bread, and all of the other clichés indicating number-one status. As soon as Larry phoned to invite Jane to the game, she suspected something other than attending a baseball game was on his mind because he had always refused to watch the Yankees play in person; in fact, whenever they were on television, Larry would rise and announce, "I've always hated the Yankees, even when they had Roger Maris." Then he would leave the room, and the Yankees would win.

Still, on the off chance that Larry was in an altered state and somehow wanted to see the Yankees in person and that was all there was to the date, Jane happily accepted Larry's proposal. Also, she is always happy to experience this peculiar Manhattan rite whereby entire families proclaim in unison that the visiting team sucks, stadium denizens on a perpetual Yankee jihad produce ticket stubs from last year's Pat Benatar concert to attempt to prove that your seat is their seat, and, while the other team is at bat, Yankee announcer Phil Rizzuto ponders the riddle of golf and why he isn't in the Hall of Fame, which is what's going on right now.

LARRY *(smiling):* Don't get too excited, Jane. Every time I go to a Yankee game, they lose. I'm a jinx and I love it.

JANE: You've never been to a Yankee game with me. They always win when I'm in the stadium.

LARRY: We'll see about that. You realize I'm actively rooting for the other team, even though the guy selling peanuts may sell me a bag laced with Drano.

JANE: At least you'll die standing for something—hating the team that produced Joe Di Maggio, Babe Ruth, Graig Nettles, Catfish—

LARRY: —Hey, all I can say is—

JANE: —I know, I know. *(in singsong voice)* George Steinbrenner has ruined baseball.

LARRY: Well, he has. How can you deny it?

JANE: Larry, how can you not just know in every cell of your body that no matter what the score is, Yankees rule? That's all there is to it.

LARRY: Maybe, but I hope your bags are packed in case you commit some sort of rooting error and there's a surprise mid-inning trade.

JANE *(getting up):* Excuse me. I'll be right back. I have to make a call.

LARRY: Who are you calling?

JANE: Trish. I had a message that she called earlier and I didn't get a chance to call her back.

LARRY: How can you get up in the middle of a Yankee game to make a phone call?

163

JANE: The other team is at bat, and even if they get a hit, they're going to lose. *(Jane dashes off.)*

LARRY *(to guy sitting next to him, not immediately noticing that he's wearing a T-shirt that says* YANKEES DO IT WHEN THEY HAVE TO.): Typical Yankee fan.

GUY: Aren't we all?

LARRY *(sizing up the guy, who isn't big, but is definitely someone who could beat Larry in arm wrestling, among other things):* Uh, I guess so.

GUY: Don't you think the other team sucks? Isn't that why you're here? Isn't that why we're all here?

LARRY: Uh, sort of. I mean, I like baseball—

GUY: Did you see that? Beautiful double play. Around the horn like Big Ben and Guidry's out of a jam, it's like get ready for the second coming. *(going crazy for a moment)* I'm talking about hallelujah and ole hot damn, we're cookin' in the pennant fryin' pan. You were saying?

LARRY: Uh, yeah, you see, I like baseball, but I'm really here because—now you're going to think this sounds kind of weird—

GUY: —Hey, I was here the day Nixon came to Yankee Stadium during Watergate, and someone spots him and he starts chanting, "Nixon sucks, Nixon sucks, Nixon sucks," and pretty soon eighty thousand people are chanting, "Nixon sucks, Nixon sucks, Nixon sucks," and Nixon can

164

barely get to his seat and the umpire calls a time out. Now *that* was weird.

LARRY: Yeah, that is pretty weird. Look, can I tell you something?

GUY: Fire away, pal.

LARRY: I'm in love with the girl I'm sitting with and she loves the Yankees, and I'm a nervous—

GUY: —Did you see that? Randolph leads off the inning with a single. He's on base with a leg injury. This is wild! The Yankees need this win and Willie knows it.

(Jane returns to her seat.)

JANE: She wasn't there. I hope she's not upset that I didn't phone back earlier.

(The guy next to Larry eyes Jane and then gives Larry the okay sign. Larry shrugs as in, "See what I mean?")

LARRY: The only person who isn't upset that you didn't phone back earlier is Ma Bell.

(But Jane is absorbed in the action.)

JANE: What?

LARRY: I said, want a Yankee frank?

JANE *(imitating old TV commercial):* "Ees great to be with a wiener." Remember that? Luis Tiant.

165

LARRY: Another Yankee putz.

(Jane and the guy sitting next to Larry both turn toward Larry.)

JANE AND GUY: Tiant? Are you kidding?

LARRY *(motioning to hot-dog peddler):* Yo! Hot dogs! Two. Over here.

GUY: Make that three.

(The hot dogs arrive and Larry pays. Jane, Larry, and the guy eat with gusto, although Larry can't refrain from using the occasion as a way to criticize the Yankees.)

LARRY: Steinbrenner must mix these with used freighter parts in order to get the most out of his money.

GUY: I think I'll have another one. *(to vendor)* Yo! Hot dogs!

(Just then the crack of a home run is heard. The crowd is on its feet as the Yankees score two runs. Jane and the guy next to Larry exchange the high five right in front of Larry.)

LARRY: Hey, pal. Hands off my girl.

GUY: Relax, man. I was just giving her the high-five.

JANE *(simultaneously upset and impressed):* Larry!

LARRY: Just kidding. I suddenly wanted to find out what it's like to be Matt.

JANE: Well, how was it?

LARRY: It's better being me, although I think I could get the hang of being Matt, the part of Matt that doesn't mind telling the world that he's got a girl.

(Jane and Larry exchange a look, hold it to the point where neither knows if it's all right to look away, neither wants to look away, and neither does, until—another crack is heard and the crowd is on its feet, roaring.)

GUY: Big Dave homers in three more runs. I don't like Winfield, to tell you the truth—too much of a company man for my taste. I mean, remember when Reggie told Steinbrenner to take a hike and then Billy Martin said one was a born liar and the other was a convicted liar and then the Yankees went on to win the whole enchilada—jeeze, that was a great time. Winfield's no straw that stirs the drink, you know what I'm saying, but he's a heck of an athlete, am I right?

(Jane and the guy high-five on this. The Yankees go down swinging, and the opposing team starts to score some runs. Jane excuses herself again to make a phone call.)

LARRY *(to guy sitting next to him):* So, what do you think? Should I go for it?

GUY: When in doubt, go for it.

LARRY: That's my instinct.

GUY: Go for what?

LARRY: The girl sitting next to me.

(The guy looks over at the seat next to Larry. It's empty.)

GUY: There's no one there.

LARRY: Hey, wise guy, she'll be back in a sec. I'm strung out here. What do you think? I mean, if I go for it, this is it.

GUY: You ever hear of a guy named Jim Morrison?

LARRY: What's that got to do with anything?

GUY *(imitating Jim Morrison):* "Love her madly."

LARRY: But he said, "Love her madly, as she's walking out the door."

GUY: So you know Jim Morrison.

LARRY: Hey, people are strange.

GUY: When you're a stranger.

LARRY: People are lonely.

GUY: When you are strange.

LARRY: All right, all right, she lights my fire.

GUY: Then like I said, pal, love her madly, even when she's walking out the door—which I hope never happens, but might, judging from the number of phone calls this broad makes.

LARRY: You noticed?

168

GUY: Hey, she's a twentieth-century fox, what can I say? I notice all chicks. If you want to spend the rest of your life in someone's soul kitchen, hers doesn't look too shabby.

LARRY: Hey, pal, that's enough advice, okay?

GUY: The Yankees and Jim Morrison, I'm a little out of control, you'll have to excuse me.

(Jane returns and takes her seat.)

JANE: Her line's busy. You know, Trish is the only civilized modern I know without call-waiting on her phone. I wish she'd wake up and smell the mochaccino.

LARRY *(wearily):* You could always have the operator butt in with one of your "medical emergencies."

JANE *(taking him seriously):* You think?

LARRY: No, I don't, actually. Just relax for a while, okay?

JANE: Okay.

(But Jane jumps up excitedly and Larry jumps up too. It's time for the seventh-inning stretch. As everyone in the stadium is singing "Take Me Out to the Ballgame," Larry pulls Jane to him.)

LARRY: Guess what?

JANE: You're pregnant?

LARRY: I got an AIDS test and I'm negative.

JANE: Without me even asking you to get one?

LARRY: Yup.

JANE: Guess what?

LARRY: You're pregnant?

JANE: I got an AIDS test too, and I'm negative.

LARRY: Without me even asking you to get one?

JANE: Yup.

LARRY: You didn't do it for someone else, did you?

JANE: Nope. Did you?

LARRY: Nope. Just for you.

JANE: Same here.

LARRY: Does that mean we can go home and I can fuck your brains out?

JANE: I promise to move like an animal.

LARRY: I promise to touch you in the right places. Let's blow this popstand before there's a new Yankee manager.

JANE: I want to stay and watch the Yankees win and hear Frank Sinatra sing the New York song.

LARRY: I'll sing it to you myself if you say you'll leave right now.

JANE: You'll sing the whole thing yourself? With your terrible voice?

LARRY: With my terrible voice.

JANE: Deal.

LARRY *(singing):* "If I can make it here, I can make it anywhere, it's up to you, New York . . ."

(The two get up to leave.)

GUY *(whispering to Larry):* Nice catch.

LARRY: She was right over the plate.

(The two men exchange the high-five unbeknownst to Jane. On the way home Larry and Jane listen to Larry's old-style transistor radio in the subway. Between bursts of static and Phil Rizzuto discussing The Hall of Fame, they hear that the Yankees lose in the tenth inning.)

LARRY: That's 'cause you left.

JANE: That's 'cause you came.

LARRY: Come here. *(pulling her close)* I want to steal a base, I mean kiss.

(They kiss passionately as the D train hurtles downtown.)

NOVEMBER

AND AWAY WE GO, AGAIN

In which Jane has her last moment flying solo.

Jane is alone in her bedroom. She is sitting in front of a mirror in her wedding gown. Although the dress fits her perfectly and she looks beautiful in it, she seems a bit distressed. She rearranges her hair and veil as her thoughts are heard in a voice-over.

JANE: This feels so strange. I'm hiding myself under a veil. Why do so many little girls have fantasies about hiding themselves under a veil? I never had this fantasy. At least I don't remember it. I remember wanting to be the ice skater on top of one of my birthday cakes. I remember wanting to play third base for the Cleveland Indians. I remember wanting to fly away by myself in a little pink plane. It's funny—I always hated pink. Except for that plane. Those fantasies—it always was me, by myself. I couldn't imagine being called "Mrs." I hope Larry doesn't want me to call myself "Mrs." I remember in high school when I told everyone I was going to college and everybody, even some of the girls, said, "Why—going after your M.R.S. degree?" Denise Gagliano had to explain what they were talking about. I guess I'm finally getting that degree. I wonder what it will be like to not just be a two-cat household. I wonder what it will be like to stop telling Trish everything. I wonder if I will. I wonder what married sex is like. No more "orgasms in a void." I bet Larry will be turned on by this gown! He loves me in white. And I must say, my ta-tas are looking rather bodacious in this push-up bra. You know, for a fantasy, maybe it's even worth being called "Mrs."

(Jane's mother enters her bedroom, a petite, healthy-looking woman in her fifties. We notice immediately that tatas, as in bodacious, run in the family.)

MOM: Yoo-hoo, Miss Blushing Bride . . .

JANE (VO): When I'm married will Mom call me Mrs. Smarty Pants?

MOM *(popping in):* Jane, dear, I hope you don't mind, but the reception is turning out to be so big that I had to cut back from three to two strawberries per glass of champagne.

JANE: That seems fine. But, just out of curiosity, why?

174

MOM: Well, as you know, your father and I haven't spoken since the divorce. Our first conversation in years was about the cost of food at your wedding. We compromised. He said he'd spring for the champagne if I'd pop for the fruit.

JANE: Mom, if you want me to chip in, just say so.

MOM: Not at your own wedding, dear. Besides, I don't want Larry's parents to think that the Lazaruses are cheap. However, as one last cost-cutting measure, I did ask the caterer to substitute one apple for every third pear in the horns of plenty. Do you think anyone will notice?

JANE: How could they? They'll be too busy counting the strawberries in their champagne.

MOM: They will?

JANE: Mom, you're making this into too big a deal. It's only a wedding. People have them all the time.

MOM: I haven't noticed anyone in this family getting married lately, have you?

JANE: All right, Mom. I'm on my way to the altar, so you can stop worrying now.

MOM: I'm your mother and I'm supposed to worry. I hope Trish doesn't get sloshed and start telling dirty jokes.

JANE: Mom, Trish can do whatever she wants at my wedding. She always figured she'd get married first, so you have to understand, she's a little upset.

175

(Just then, Dad swaggers in, martini in hand.)

DAD *(stiffly, to Mom):* Hello, Miriam.

MOM *(similarly):* Hello, Frank. *(to Jane)* I better go make sure your sister is ironing those napkins properly. See you at the rehearsal dinner, Miss Growing-Up-Right-Before-My-Eyes.

JANE: Mom, I'm thirty-six years old!

MOM: You'll always be my little baby in the stroller with the raccoon hat. Oooh, *(tweaking Jane's cheeks)* you were so cute, I could almost cry.

(Dad hands Mom a handkerchief. She takes the hanky.)

DAD: Miriam, you look like you could use a martooni.

MOM *(sniffling):* No thanks. If I dilly-dally now, I'll miss my two o'clock conference with the florist.

(Mom rushes off, crying loudly now.)

DAD: I think she's taking it like a trouper, don't you?

JANE: Well, I don't think she's cried enough to qualify for the Guinness Book of Records, but check with me again tomorrow.

DAD: Feel like a little martooni?

JANE: No, thanks.

DAD *(sipping):* So how's my best girl?

JANE: Fine.

DAD: Are you sure? Come on, you can tell the old man. Remember those great talks we used to have?

JANE: What talks?

DAD: On the way to Sunday school, remember?

JANE: You mean when we used to take the long way home so we could play the license plate game?

DAD: Remember the time you spotted that pickup truck from New Mexico—

JANE: —Land of Enchantment—

DAD: —and I promised that someday I'd take you to New Mexico so you could see the enchanted land?

JANE: Sort of.

DAD: Jane, I have to tell you something. I failed as your father. I never took you to see the Land of Enchantment.

JANE: Dad, that's ridiculous. You took me to a lot of great places—there were those rocks in the shape of Winston Churchill and . . . those rocks were great, Dad. Really.

DAD: Seriously?

JANE: Seriously. I wouldn't have wanted to go to see rocks in the shape of Winston Churchill with any other Dad.

(A beat.)

DAD: Now, Jane. If you're having second thoughts about spending the rest of your life with Larry whatever his name is, you can always back out now. It's not too late.

JANE: Dad! I love Larry!

DAD: A little while ago, you came to me and did not speak too highly of anyone who answered to the name of Larry.

JANE: I was being silly.

(Dad reaches into his pocket and hands Jane an envelope.)

DAD: Here's that loan you asked for.

JANE: Dad, I don't need it now.

DAD: You never know. Keep it, take a friend out to lunch.

JANE: Well, it is a nice chunk of mad money.

DAD *(puzzled):* I'm not giving that to you because I'm mad, if that's what you mean.

JANE *(smiling):* It isn't and I know, Dad.

DAD: Anyway, this thing between you and Larry is not yet written in stone. You want to leave town—I'll put you on the next plane.

JANE: Dad, please! I want to marry Larry!

DAD: All right. You're over twenty-one. I can't stop you.

JANE: Dad, you'll like Larry.

DAD: How can I? He's stealing my best girl.

JANE: He likes Jackie Gleason.

DAD: Seriously?

JANE: Seriously.

DAD: I'm not sure I really believe you.

JANE: Well, he likes that you like Jackie Gleason. As Trish and I used to say, he groks it.

DAD: Okay, then he won't mind if I fire up the fattest stogie this side of Castro's beard at my best girl's wedding.

JANE: No, he won't mind. And neither will I.

(They hug.)

DAD: Jane, tomorrow would you mind if we took the long way to the chapel?

JANE: No, but if I spot a New Mexico plate, I'm going to take you up on that Land of Enchantment offer. *(doing Jackie Gleason imitation)* "And away we go!"

(They hug again.)

DAD: Baby, you're the greatest!

JANE: I think it's time for that martooni.

NOVEMBER
a bit later

JANE AND LARRY UP IN A TREE

In which the two young moderns branch out, turn over a new leaf, and squirrel around like a couple of nuts.

It is just after the wedding. Larry and Jane are sprawled across the floor in front of the threshold of Jane's bedroom. They are here because the entrance to Larry's bedroom in his loft is blocked by drying canvases. Jane's dress is above her hips, her underpants are not down around her ankles or anywhere else because she didn't wear any to her wedding, but she is still wearing her veil, which now is slightly askew. Larry, on top of Jane, is still wearing the top half of his tux, and one leg of the pants, but metaphysically speaking is having an out-of-suit experience.

JANE *(sighing):* Larry.

LARRY *(sighing):* Jane.

JANE *(sighing more profoundly):* Larry.

LARRY *(sighing equally):* Jane.

JANE: Oh, Larry.

LARRY: Oh, Jane.

JANE: Her master's voice. I could almost come again, just hearing you say my name.

LARRY: Other Larrys, take a hike. She's only talking to me now.

JANE: You're the only Larry I ever called out "Larry" for during sex. You're the only Larry I didn't fantasize about other Larrys with during sex. You're the only Larry. *(A beat.)* Oh, Larry.

(Larry stirs against Jane, scoops her up, and carries her into the bedroom across the threshold of a new life about which, she thinks to herself, "no more orgasms in a void". Larry tenderly puts Jane down on the bed, lifts up the veil with one hand and holds Jane around her small waist with the other, getting a firm hold against her hip. Jane's fingers creep under Larry's shirt and up to his chest, finding the tangle of hair that she is now lost in forever. Larry kisses

Jane and starts to work his chest, pawing and kneading the furry mat.)

JANE: I feel like a cat who finally got back home.

LARRY: You're starting to move like an animal.

JANE: You're starting to touch me in the right places.

LARRY *(pushing Jane back against the bed):* Like here in your pussy?

(Jane starts to make the unintelligible sounds of pleasure, words which will soon consist either entirely of vowels or consonants.)

LARRY: Like here behind your knees? *(Jane makes more sounds.)* Like here in your belly button? *(Larry's tongue follows his hands as he touches every part of Jane's body. Jane emits low rumbles like a baby tiger and climbs on top of Larry now, with nothing on but her veil. She continues to stake her claim, wrapping her fingers through the web of hair, finding Larry's collarbone, grabbing on to it and kissing him deeply while she hunkers down on his stiffer-than-the-first-time-they-did-it cock. With one hand, Larry takes Jane's waist, helping her rock against him, and puts the other low on her belly.)*

JANE: I'm burning, I'm on fire, I'm burning, I'm on fire . . .

LARRY: I love feeling your heat . . .

(Jane comes first, about a million times.)

JANE: I can't stop coming.

(Then Larry explodes too, with a shout of ecstasy that hits all the tones. After a while, Jane rolls off of Larry and wriggles into his arms, her back to his chest. He lifts up her veil so that they are both under it and they fall asleep. Some time later, Jane wakes up. She hears a familiar voice, but can't quite identify it at first.)

VOICE: That was lovely, Jane.

JANE: What?

VOICE: You kids really know how to get down.

JANE *(realizing):* Grandma, what are you doing here?

GRANDMA: Sssh. Let's not wake Larry. He's so cute when he's sleeping.

JANE *(getting up from bed and attempting to locate the source of the voice):* What're you, nuts? You're spying on my sex life?

GRANDMA: It's not just you, it's a lot of people.

JANE: Don't you have anything else to do?

GRANDMA: Well, Sol's playing poker tonight, and so I just thought—

JANE: —You thought you'd invade my privacy?

GRANDMA: Like I said, it's not just you. Last week, I watched Warren Beatty and some bimbo he picked up at a fund-raiser for Gary Hart.

JANE *(curious):* How was it?

(Jane locates the source of the voice. It's the radiator.)

GRANDMA: It was good for me, but I don't know about her. I don't think he could find her F stop.

JANE: G spot.

GRANDMA: Well, you know what I mean. Anyway, I just wanted to stop by and offer you all the best.

JANE: You sound like a clergyman.

GRANDMA: That's another thing that happens when you die.

JANE *(amused):* So you really like Larry, huh?

GRANDMA: Even though he's the only Larry in the world who isn't a Yankee fan, I think you got yourself a real jewel there.

JANE: Thank you.

GRANDMA: And that hair on his chest—is he some kind of piece of work, or what?

JANE: Grandma!

GRANDMA: Sorry. Like I told you, Sol's playing poker to-night, and I'm a little lonely, what can I tell you?

JANE: Grandma, can I ask you a question?

GRANDMA: Not to put too fine a point on it, but I think I can spare a few minutes.

JANE: Will this last forever?

GRANDMA: Yes. You want to hear some more lies? Life's a beach. Johnny Carson is the funniest man on the planet. With age comes wisdom. So what do I know?

JANE: Plenty, Grandma.

GRANDMA: Excuse me, I hear Sol pulling up in the Corvair.

JANE: Drop in any time, but preferably when I'm alone.

GRANDMA: Okay, but remember, heat attracts ghosts. That's why I'm in here, although to tell you the truth, radiators don't really do it for me. So next time you make like two pieces of flint, I may stop by to check out the action.

JANE: Well, I hope Sol keeps you busier than that. Tell him I said hello. You know, he's got a real jewel there.

GRANDMA: Thank you, dear.

JANE: Bye, Grandma.

(She lies back down next to Larry, curls up, and goes to sleep, the two of them now like a pair of spoons.)

DECEMBER

LUNCH #3

In which Trish and Jane ponder the secret
meaning of this ancient female ceremony.

It is now one week after Jane's wedding. Trish and Jane
are at their favorite tearoom. They are both a little nervous about seeing each other, wondering privately how
Jane's marital status will affect their friendship. But after
a couple of glasses of champagne it is clear that they will
forever be girls in suits at lunch, despite the fact that for
the first time in her lunching life, Trish is not wearing a
suit.

TRISH *(draining her first glass of champagne):* So . . .
is it true? Is married sex better?

JANE: I can't talk about it. I promised Larry I wouldn't go public with our private lives.

TRISH: Wait. Am I having lunch with Jane Lazarus or a bad impostor?

JANE: What about me? I barely recognize you without the power shoulders.

TRISH: Well, now that I'm actively dating, or trying to, I figured it might be a good idea to eighty-six the suit, and let men *(eyeing Jack, the waiter)* see a bit more of me.

JANE: I'm sure they'll agree, Trish—you have lovely shoulders, even without the Marc Gastiheau pads.

(They both laugh.)

JANE: Well, it's a new me, too, that's for sure. I feel that it would be a total violation of the sanctity of marriage for me to start describing every intimate detail of what goes on in the conjugal futon.

TRISH *(disappointed):* Well, okay.

(She motions to waiter for another round.)

JANE *(disappointed):* Aren't you even going to try and drag something out of me?

TRISH: No. I respect what you're saying, and I won't do it.

JANE: You're a good friend, Trish.

(A beat.)

JANE *(excitedly):* Want to know what happened on our wedding night? I can't keep it to myself any longer. On the way to the airport in the limo, just as we were entering the Holland Tunnel—

TRISH: Jane! You don't have to tell me! I don't want to know! It's not my business!

(A beat.)

JANE: I'm sorry I was the one who got married first. I know it wasn't supposed to happen this way.

(Trish starts crying.)

TRISH: I'm sorry. I'm actually happy for you. But I'm also hurt, jealous, and angry.

JANE: Hey, I would be too.

TRISH: I guess I feel so *single.* I'm turning into one of these women you read about—attractive, accomplished, witty, warm, wise, fun; she did it her way and now . . . she's steaming vegetables for one.

JANE: But, Trish, you've never actually been alone. You've always had a fella when you've wanted one.

TRISH: True.

JANE: What's going on with Chris?

TRISH: He's so wrapped up with the Rolexes-for-toddlers campaign, I hardly ever get to see him.

189

JANE: Well, don't be too hard on him. Look at us. I was going to use the five thousand dollars my father gave me and take us to Paris for lunch, but you canceled out because of the parking meter scandal.

TRISH: Gee, I'm sorry. I've been so busy taking depositions from corrupt politicians, I haven't even had time to get my legs waxed.

(Jane looks underneath the table at Trish's legs.)

JANE: No kidding.
(They laugh, pouncing on the moment a little too avidly, grateful for the first bit of lunchtime fun.)

JANE: Well, the truth is, I probably would have canceled out myself. I'm so caught up in my new manuscript that even during my honeymoon I was making notes on the joke cocktail napkins.

TRISH: Your honeymoon involved joke cocktail napkins?

JANE: Not really.

TRISH: I know, I know. You just like the phrase.

JANE: But I did make a lot of notes.

TRISH *(checking her watch):* We've been here for fifteen minutes and you haven't even gotten up once to make a phone call. I don't know if I can get used to this kind of uninterrupted lunch.

JANE: Well, I suppose I could get up and go call Larry. Just for old time's sake.

TRISH: I'm just teasing.

JANE: On second thought, maybe I better phone him. He might think I'm taking him for granted if I don't.

TRISH: Gee, you're always so suggestible. Sometimes I wonder what else I can get you to do besides make phone calls.

JANE: If your back weren't so small, probably a lot. I'll be right back.

(She gets up and heads for the telephone. Jack, Manhattan's last heterosexual waiter, approaches.)

JACK: So, Robert Chambers: Guilty or innocent?

TRISH: Now, that is one guy who is definitely guilty.

JACK: Of what? Finally being unable to take one more meaningless encounter with another faceless member of the testosterone-crazed female throng?

TRISH: Jack, have you lost a few tiles on reentry?

JACK: That's what I hear.

TRISH: Are you saying the "preppy murderer" is innocent?

JACK *(being flagged by another table)*: Excuse me. *(then, loudly)* By the way, you never phoned.

191

(Jane returns. An assortment of tea sandwiches arrive, and the girls make a selection from the cart.)

TRISH: What is it about these sandwiches that's so comforting?

JANE: I don't know. I remember my first tea sandwich. I was with my grandmother. We were at the Bird Cage restaurant in Lord and Taylor. There were lots of grandmothers and granddaughters. *(in girlish voice)* It was a real big treat for all of us. Then afterward we had triple chocolate sundaes with lots of those tiny marshmallows.

TRISH: My first tea sandwich was at a tea party my mother was having. I remember being so excited because there were all these sandwich triangles without the crusts! The best one was the tuna salad. I took mine back into the kitchen, peeled back the date-nut bread, and added potato chips because that was the best way to eat a tuna salad sandwich.

(Another beat passes as they eat, and sip their champagne.)

TRISH: I just want you to know that your wedding was quite something.

JANE: Thank you.

TRISH: You know, I've never been to a Jewish wedding before, and quite frankly, I really didn't know what to expect.

192

JANE: Did you think that we get hepped up on Manischewitz and make prank phone calls to the Archbishop of Canterbury and say things like, "Do you have Prince Albert in the can?"

TRISH: Hey, don't get me wrong. Your wedding was really nice.

JANE: Nice? That's all you have to say?

TRISH: Well, I loved the part where Larry serenaded you with "My Girl," even though he has a terrible voice.

JANE *(misty-eyed):* It's hard to top the Temptations for schmaltz.

TRISH: What is "schmaltz," exactly? I never really knew. I mean "oy" I know, and "kitsch," I know what that means . . .

JANE: Trish, "kitsch" doesn't have anything to do with Judaism—linguistically, that is. But I've always suspected that there's a suppressed edition of the Old Testament that says, "In the beginning was the word and the word was schmaltz." Of course, the traditionally vowel-fearing Hasids dropped the "a" but that's another story. Anyway, "schmaltz" is, uh, "schmaltz" is kind of like the end of most television shows when everybody phones their relatives, or, in real life, any moment that could be backed up by a pair of castanets.

TRISH *(pondering this):* That's what I thought.

(A beat.)

TRISH: And I liked it when you and your father did the Charleston, even though he's a terrible dancer.

JANE *(starting to become suspicious):* Yeah?

TRISH: But to tell you the truth, I wasn't wild about the part where the bride and groom step on the wineglass. I mean, all that commotion in the middle of a wedding ceremony.

JANE: There wasn't any commotion.

TRISH: Well, I suppose it's a colorful ritual.

JANE *(becoming more suspicious):* Trish, you better get that suit jacket out of the dry cleaner's. You sound like Emily Post on bad acid. *(imitating her)* "And the unnecessary breakage practiced by the Hebrews? Oh my!"

TRISH: Well, it's just that . . .

(She bursts into tears. Jane immediately takes her hand.)

JANE: What is it, Trish?

TRISH *(sniffling):* Jane, I didn't catch the bouquet.

JANE: Yeah, but your mother did, and she needs to get married more than you do.

TRISH: If she marries this guy she's been dating, I'll have a Vietnam vet for a stepfather—

JANE: —and when the minister says, "Speak now or forever hold your peace," you can jump up and yell, "Ho, Ho, Ho Chi Minh, NLF is gonna win."

(Trish starts laughing through her tears. Then Jane starts to laugh too. They both laugh a lot, grateful for the moment.)

TRISH: When we were majoring in striking and chanting, did you ever think that any of the things that have happened to us would happen?

JANE: I didn't have a clue. I always knew I wanted to write, but . . . *(suddenly getting worried)* I hope I can write when I'm pregnant.

TRISH: Why not? You can make notes on your blood sugar readouts.

JANE: What if I get pregnant and like it so much that I give up writing and turn into Ethel Kennedy?

TRISH: Somehow I don't think that's the hand you've been dealt, Jane.

JANE: You're probably right, Trish. When I get knocked up, I don't want to spend nine months grinning like a moron. I can't stand women who do that. And when junior issues forth, I want to be out like Sunny von Bülow. No Lamaze for this gal. Why does everybody get so worried about what kind of birth they're having as opposed to what they're going to do with the kid for the next eighteen years?

TRISH: Dr. Spock turned us into a generation obsessed with birth methods.

JANE: Well, color me comatose. I hope Larry doesn't mind. But he probably will. You know, he actually knows the days that I'm ovulating. I don't, but he does.

TRISH: You got yourself a good catch there, Jane. I hope you never forget that. And he's kind of a lucky so-and-so himself.

JANE: Thanks. Maybe I'll go tell him right now.

(Jane gets up and heads for the telephone.)

TRISH *(muttering to herself as she checks her watch):* Old Faithful.

(Jack notices that Trish is alone, and approaches again.)

JACK: Okay, so I came on like gangbusters.

TRISH: Did I say I minded?

JACK: No, but you didn't phone.

TRISH: Well, the truth is, I'm seriously involved with someone.

JACK: Who—your lunch mate?

TRISH: So now I'm a dyke because I didn't phone?

JACK: Sorry, I was just teasing. Let's start over. If Robert Chambers came to you and asked you to defend him—

196

TRISH: That is one case I would turn down. What about you?

JACK: I'd ask him about his pickup techniques.

TRISH: You don't have to ask him to know what they are. Give her a couple of mixed drinks on a hot summer night, take her behind a museum, have sex that involves the unusual placement of underpants, and then—

JACK: —another lady-killer. You said Claus von Bülow was charming. Why draw the line with him?

TRISH: I didn't say that. A friend said that. Anyway, for a guy who knows what sort of brassiere I prefer, just because he serves me lunch occasionally, I think you're becoming far too presumptuous.

JACK: Not presumptuous enough. What are you doing next Saturday?

TRISH *(flustered):* I'm, uh, well—

JACK *(rushing off to another table):* I'd like to continue this Robert Chambers discussion in, shall we say, more private chambers.

(Jane returns. Trish is extremely distracted.)

JANE: What's going on?

TRISH: Our waiter just asked me out.

JANE: You seem displeased.

TRISH: Just confused. I think I'm in love with Chris, but . . .

JANE: You sound like me.

TRISH: I told you. *(indicating shoulders)* No suit. More dating. Somebody has to pick up the baton of serial excitement.

JANE: Well, don't rush into anything. Give it at least another fifteen or twenty minutes.

TRISH: To tell you the truth, I'm not so sure how involved I could ever get with a dropout lawyer.

JANE: Don't you actually mean a "waiter"?

TRISH: I suppose maybe I do.

JANE: How would you like it if you were a waitress, in every other respect still yourself, and one day you waited on this cute guy, and you struck up this little friendship based on friction, and whenever he came in you started talking about current events, especially as they related to law, because he was a lawyer, and you were once too, but you were now a waitress because the legal profession had sent you into a deep depression in which the line between good and evil was severely blurred, so you had dropped out, and now this cute guy wants to go out with you but even though you're smart, witty, and attractive, he won't because after all, you're only a waitress?

TRISH: I'd never be in that position.

JANE: Come on, Trish. Think about it. You and I have always hated that kind of class discrimination. Women have always been on the receiving end of it. I thought everything was different now.

TRISH: It is different—and it's all the same.

JANE: Maybe you should give him just a teeny-tiny chance? Don't you want to try out your new suit-free look?

TRISH: Hey, you know me. I make the longest opening arguments in legal—and dating—history. But then *(with great relish)* when the drama unfolds . . .

JANE: It's a sensible M.O.

TRISH: *Nolo contendere,* I guess. *(A beat.)* So, do you think you'll get pregnant right away?

JANE: If I wait any longer, I might be attending my potential offspring's school play in an iron lung.

TRISH: Meanwhile, my biological clock is ticking away. God, I loathe that expression, "biological clock." It sounds so New York *Times Magazine.*

JANE: I know. Back in the old days, like last week, I imagined when I was out on a date, there was this gigantic, ticking grandfather clock right next to the dinner table, and as dinner progressed, the ticking got louder and louder and soon my date would hear it. *(dramatically)* Then he'd turn to me and say, "What's that ticking?" and I'd have to say, "Ticking? I don't hear any ticking," but the ticking would get louder and louder, like Captain Hook, and just as we were about to finish dinner, an alarm would go off, like this—

199

(imitating screeching) all over town, even people in the subway could hear it, and then I'd have to say, "Oh, sorry. My biological clock. It just went off. I hope I didn't embarrass you. I thought I had everything under control."

(Trish and Jane laugh at this, a bit drunkenly now.)

TRISH *(lifting glass in toast):* Well, here's to our clocks.

JANE *(toasting):* May they never stop ticking.

TRISH: I'll drink to that.

(They swill down the rest of their champagne, motion for another round, and ask for the check. Their drinks arrive.)

JANE *(eyeing Jack):* This time I'm sure of it. He is the last heterosexual waiter in Manhattan.

TRISH: It won't last. Even Hulk Hogan would lose it after serving forty thousand orders of *oeufs à la neige.*
(They giggle. The check arrives. Jane goes to pick it up, but Trish puts her hand on top of Jane's.)

TRISH: I thought I was taking you out?

JANE: No, the five thousand dollars, remember? I'm putting it into our lifetime lunch fund.

TRISH: But we're celebrating your first week of state-certified cohabitation.

JANE: I thought we were celebrating your new Italian office furniture.

200

TRISH: Jane, look. I still remember when you were a starving writer. You lived off the snacks at press parties. Remember the time you wolfed down an entire barrel of chicken wings at that hoedown for the Isley Brothers?

JANE *(a bit embarrassed):* Sort of. Hey, remember when you were taking your law boards and you were living on that weird work-study ration of Seven-Up and Mars bars?

TRISH *(grabbing the check):* Never in a million years did I subsist on a diet of cheap toxins. Look, I want to pay.

(She looks at it, but Jane peers over and looks too.)

JANE: How much is it?

TRISH and JANE: Let's split it.

(They open up their purses to retrieve the cash, but can't find their wallets, and end up emptying the contents of their respective handbags onto the table, item by item.)

TRISH: Sorry, I don't have any cash.

JANE: Me neither.

TRISH: I'll just put it on my Diner's Club.

JANE: That's what I was going to do.

TRISH *(calling out):* Excuse me, waiter, could you split this check in half? *(to Jane)* Should I have said, "Excuse me, Jack"?

JANE: You know me. Jane "Why stand on formality?" Lazarus.

TRISH: So you are keeping your last name.

JANE: Gee, I haven't even thought about *that*. I'm sure I will. When the kid's old enough, he or she can decide between Lazarus and Kallachinsky.

TRISH: Obviously, you did not marry Larry for his last name.

(Jack arrives and splits the check.)

JACK *(to Trish)*: For the record, counselor, I want it known that even though I've served over fifty thousand orders of braised shiitake mushrooms, I still haven't lost it.

(He walks off without waiting for a reaction.)

TRISH: Interesting.

JANE: Bold.

TRISH: Interesting and bold.

(They each pay their own checks, and then hurriedly prepare to leave.)

JANE: Trish, I have a request. Would you promise me one thing?

TRISH: Sure.

JANE: No matter what's going on in our lives, can we always have lunch?

TRISH: Till death do us part?

(The girls hug.)

TRISH/JANE: Now, that's schmaltz.

JANE: Or maybe it's kitsch.

TRISH: By the way, Jane, how come you're not wearing your ring?

JANE: I don't want anyone to call me "Mrs."

(Trish and Jane leave the restaurant, and disappear into the midday Manhattan swirl.)

203

ABOUT THE AUTHOR

Deanne Stillman is the author of *Getting Back at Dad,* the co-author of *Woodstock Census: The Nationwide Survey of the 60s Generation, Titters 101, The Mom Book,* and the co-editor of *Titters: The First Collection of Humor by Women.* Her articles appear in many magazines, including the *Village Voice, GQ, New York Woman, Redbook, Glamour, Playboy,* and *Mademoiselle,* to which she is a contributing editor. Her work has been anthologized in *Mass Media* and in *Audition.* Deanne also writes for television, including the series "Square Pegs," "The New Gidget," and "A Different World."